Inheritance

A Quill Gordon Mystery

Michael Wallace

ISBN: 978-0-615-68434-5

Acknowledgements

No one writes a book alone, and that is certainly true of this one. Several people have provided suggestions and direction along the way, and in that regard I would particularly like to thank Denise Marcil, Bud O'Brien and Melissa Milich. Every author needs help with technical matters. I thank William F. Locke-Paddon for suggestions on preparing a challengeable will and to Gary Wollin for advice on playing the stock market. If I got something wrong in either of those areas, the fault is mine, not theirs. And last but not least thanks to my wife, Linda, for her patience, understanding and support during all those hours I was isolated with the computer writing this novel.

No one markets a book alone, either, and thanks are due in that area as well. I am indebted to to John Bakalian for his tireless research into e-book publication and publicity; Deborah Karas for designing a bold and striking book cover; to Chip Scheuer and Rigo Torkos for creating a dynamic and eye-catching video; to Greg Pio, photographer, for making me look better than I really do; to Karen Kefauver for her invaluable help with social media promotion; to Melody Sharp for coming up with a clean and useful web site; and to intellectual property attorney Michael Mount for helping protect my legal rights.

In the spirit of Dornford Yates,

For Linda and Bud

The Angler and the Sharpshooter

Squinting into the early morning sun, the angler cast a practiced eye at the creek winding through the meadow before him. After fishing it for 25 years, he knew the water by heart and had a memory to go with every riffle, every pool, every bend. The weeks following Labor Day, with summer fast yielding to autumn, were often the best of the season. Sensing the approach of winter, the fish began to feed with abandon. A large attractor fly cast just short of the deeply undercut grassy banks could yield a sudden and violent strike on the surface of the water, followed by a scrappy fight with an energetic trout.

Taking cover behind a clump of sagebrush to keep a low profile from the fish, the angler planned his cast. He was standing at a bend in the creek, which cut a deep channel against the opposite side. With a good cast to the current at the head of the bend, and a quick upstream mend of his line after the fly had drifted ten feet, he could get a clean drift over twenty feet of water that, by all reckoning, should be holding some good fish. The cast had to be precise, however. Too long, and he could find himself tangled in the grass or brush on the opposite shore; too short and the fly would sit still on the dead water in the middle.

He was holding the fly, a size 12 Royal Wulff, in his hand. Later in the day he would switch to a grasshopper pattern, but it was too early now. With his left hand, the angler tossed the fly out over the water then stripped several feet of his line from the reel and began to cast. He made several false casts, admiring the tightness of the loop his line was making, then let the line shoot forward and fall lightly on the water. The fly landed just where he wanted, and he held his breath as it drifted downstream with the current. He executed the upstream mend and got the perfect 20-foot drift. His audience, the fish, let it pass.

A hundred yards behind him, entirely obscured by trees and brush, the sharpshooter lifted a deer rifle and sighted the angler in its crosshairs. With no obstructions and a still target, it would have been an easy shot, but the angler was in a direct line with the sun, which threw a blinding glare into the rifle's telescopic lens. The sharpshooter cursed silently. This was not something that anyone would want to linger over, but there was nothing for it but to wait until the angler moved up or down stream enough to get out of the line of the sun. Gripped with feelings of irritation, impatience and anxiety, the sharpshooter lowered the rifle.

Meanwhile, the angler had made another perfect cast without a fish. Setting his rod down, he knelt on the grass and stuck a hand into the creek. The water was cold, probably in the low fifties — maybe just a little too cold for the fish to be looking for food on the surface. He turned and looked behind him at the few patches of frost remaining in the meadow. Although he did not know it, he was looking right in the direction of the sharpshooter.

Shaking the water off his hand, he considered his options. He could fish beneath the surface with a nymph and probably catch a few fish now, but the prospect held little interest for him. It was so much more exciting to take a fish on the dry fly, where you could see it strike, sometimes even see it coming out of nowhere to do so. It brought an element of the personal to angling that he felt was missing in the anonymous strikes you got on a nymph. He decided to leave the dry fly on and wait for the water to warm up.

He also decided to move downstream, where the sun had already been on the meadow longer. As he walked he looked closely at the dew on the grass, listened to the shivering of the pine trees as a short gust of wind came up and sighed through them, and took a deep breath of the clean mountain air — so familiar, yet so different from what he was used to in San Francisco. He found himself overcome by a feeling of profound sadness as these familiar things brought home how much this place meant to him. About 150 feet from the bend where he had been casting, he stopped and looked out over the creek. The sun was now almost directly to his right, and he cast a long shadow along the edge of the bank.

Perfect, thought the sharpshooter, raising the deer rifle again. The glare was gone and it was easy to get a clean sighting. Looking through the telescopic lens, the sharpshooter aimed the crosshairs directly at the middle of the back of the angler's head and held them there for half a minute before thinking, "He's still now, but he could move his head any time, and I don't want to shoot twice." Lowering the crosshairs, the sharpshooter traced a line down the angler's neck and spine, stopping a third of the way down and moving a little to the left, where the heart should be. It was an easy shot. The sharpshooter took a deep breath and stayed in place with the finger precisely on the trigger. A gentle squeeze and it's over. A minute later there had been no squeeze, and the rifle was lowered.

He had been seven years old, the angler remembered, when his father first took him out here with a bag of worms and a cheap spinning rod. As is often the case with small boys, he had been lucky. A worm, drifted to a deep hole, had been grabbed by a 14-inch rainbow trout, and he recalled with pride how he had fought the fish himself while his father stood by beaming, then finally netted it. They cooked the fish for dinner that night and he shared it with his sister.

A lot had changed since then. He now fished with a fly rod and released the fish he caught, but that was the least of it. It had been a long time since he enjoyed his father's approval and now, with the old man dead, there was no chance he ever would. Why had they done it to him, his father and sister? Granted, he was different, at least by their standards. He had known that very early on in life, even though it took a while to realize why. And they assured him it didn't make any difference, but he didn't believe them. After all, what else could it be?

The sharpshooter lifted the rifle again and took aim. As still as the angler was standing, it was almost like shooting at a target. That's it, thought the sharpshooter.

Think of it as shooting at a target, or a deer. His death would mean less to the world than the passing of a deer and might even do some good. God knows he's caused enough pain already.

It took an almost physical effort for the angler to stop brooding and will himself into fishing again. Where he was standing, the creek ran for about 75 feet in a straight channel between grassy, overhanging banks. The bottom rose to a slight crest a foot from the surface in the middle, but a slightly faster current ran over two feet of water by the undercut bank on the opposite side. The angler had caught fish here before. He stripped out some line, made a couple of false casts, then dropped the fly on the water six inches from the opposite shore. Yes! he thought as he watched it drift downstream. That's it. Come on. Come on. Come on. Now. Now.

Ka-chow.

Rocketing out from underneath the bank, a 12-inch Brown Trout took the fly with a splashy grab. In the three quarters of a second between then and the firing of the deer rifle, the angler raised his arm and pulled the rod back to set the hook. That accounted for the rod being dropped on the creek bank while the angler tumbled forward into the water, which began to carry his body slowly downstream. The fish thrashed around for half a minute, but with no one holding the rod and putting pressure on the line, it was finally able to throw the hook and swim back to freedom.

The gunshot had rung out like a thunderclap, reverberating through the small mountain valley. The coroner's report said that the angler had probably barely registered the sound before he was dead from a high-caliber bullet that entered his body under the left shoulder from behind and slightly above, tore out 40 percent of his heart, shattered two ribs, and ricocheted to the right, coming to rest just under the sternum. What the report didn't say was that the angler had died with a fish on.

Thursday September 9, 1993

A sudden afternoon thunderstorm had driven Quill Gordon off the East Buchanan River and into the Summit County Courthouse in Harperville. The county courthouse might seem like an unusual place for a 34-year-old stockbroker on a fishing vacation to take refuge, but Gordon had his reasons. He had an above-average level of general curiosity, which was coupled with an interest in the law that came from being the son of a judge. More to the point, in this particular case, there was a woman involved.

As Gordon stood dripping in the lobby of the courthouse, he looked around and tried to gain his bearings. Summit County takes its name from the fact that its western boundary follows the divide of the Sierra Nevada. The county seat is named after Jacob Harper, a pioneer settler who was perhaps best known for having built a bridge over the East Buchanan River two miles out of town and charging a ten-cent toll for its use. It was a lucrative enterprise, but the business ended suddenly one afternoon when a drunken cowhand took umbrage at the tariff and expressed his sentiments with firearms. After Harper had been buried for a respectable period of time there was talk of renaming the town, but as often happens in such cases, no one could agree on an alternative and the idea was eventually dropped.

Wedged between the mountains and the Nevada border, Summit County is accessible from the California side through two steep and winding passes, one of which is closed for the winter. In the 1880s, a brief gold rush swelled its population to 20,000, but by the 1890 census, 18,504 of those souls had moved on. In the 1920s, the discovery of a rich vein of silver led to another boom, which ended just in time for the county to hibernate through the Great Depression. In 1990, the county had a population of 4,037, with the primary sources of personal income being cattle ranching, tourism, working for the state highway department, and Social Security checks mailed to recently arrived retirees.

The Summit County courthouse was built during the silver boom, and its grandeur reflected the temporary prosperity of the time. The exterior was made of massive limestone blocks, and inside the floors were marble. There were two courtrooms on the second floor, one of which had been converted to a general meeting room after the boom ended. Visitors were generally struck by the brightness of the lobby, illuminated through a windowed dome by the strong mountain light. A set of stairs ran from the center of the lobby to the second story, rimmed by balconies that hovered over the entryway on three sides.

Having figured out from the directory by the doorway where the court room was, Gordon walked across the lobby, his hiking boots squeaking against the marble with every step. As he went slowly up the stairs, he appreciated the fine quality of the oak banisters, noting at the same time that they were badly in need of polishing. At the door to the courtroom he removed his dripping parka and, seeing no place to put it, slung it under his arm. As quietly as he could, he turned the knob of the door and walked in, his boots making four loud squeaks against the marble as he walked to an aisle seat in the third row from the front.

The witness being sworn in at the moment looked up briefly at the intrusion, then finished his oath and sat down. He was a man of medium height with a paunch whose age might have been anywhere between 50 and 65. The little hair on his head was gray and closely cropped, and his gray eyes gave an impression of vulnerability, rather than hardness. Wearing a sport coat with lapels a bit too wide and checks a bit too pronounced and fidgeting in his chair, he had the look of a chemistry teacher who had inexplicably been asked to give a lecture on physics.

When Gordon looked to his right, he saw that the witness had grounds for concern. Rising to examine for the plaintiff was Manfred Bosso, one of San Francisco's foremost trial lawyers. When not leaning over to get closer to a witness, Bosso stood six feet four and weighed 250 pounds. His size alone would have made him a formidable presence in the courtroom, and the impression was further enhanced by a full head of wavy white hair over a florid face with bushy eyebrows. Bosso had penetrating eyes and a deep, rolling voice that in a trial were weapons unto themselves. He had been known to strike fear into the hearts of police chiefs and the most tyrannical of business executives. Gordon guessed that the suit Bosso wore cost two thousand dollars minimum, and that he could easily afford it. Someone obviously wanted to win this trial very badly.

Sitting next to Bosso was a man about Gordon's age. That must be the brother, he thought, as his eyes moved to the other side of the aisle where Ellen McHenry was sitting with her attorney. Gordon found himself hoping her lawyer had the facts on his side, even though, against Bosso, that wasn't always enough.

"Please state your name and occupation," Bosso said, with an edge in his voice.

"My name is Howard Marchand, and I practice law in this town."

"How long have you done so?"

"Since 1962,"

"And do you number the McHenry family among your clients."

"Not at this time."

"Have you previously?"

"I represented the late Frank McHenry on a number of occasions."

"Did any of those occasions involve drawing a will for him?"

"Yes, sir."

"And how many times did you prepare a will for Frank McHenry?"

"Three times in all."

"When was the first?"

"It was in 1975, I believe."

"Could you tell the court, in general terms, what its provisions were with respect to disposing with the bulk of the estate."

"The bulk of the estate, then as now, consisted of Twin Creek Ranch and its assets, along with lease holds on various Forest Service and Bureau of Land Management lands. When that first will was drawn, Mr. McHenry's wife was still alive, and the property was left to her in trust, then to the two children in a residual trust."

"You said to the two children. Was it left to them equally?"

"No, it was not."

"How, then, was it divided?"

"The ranch itself was left to the son ..."

"That would be the plaintiff, Daniel McHenry?"

"Correct. He was to inherit the ranch and assets, and an arrangement was made for his sister, Ellen, to receive a portion of the annual earnings and to maintain living privileges on the property and free and full use of the ranch and its facilities for the remainder of her life."

"Is that, in your experience, a common way of disposing of such an estate?"

"I wouldn't say it was common, but it certainly was not unheard of at that time. And I should add that an attorney in this county doesn't see many estates such as this."

"Did you, as Mr. McHenry's attorney, recommend this arrangement to him?"

"I recommended the specifics of the trust and the formal wording with respect to the disposition."

"Let me rephrase the question. Whose idea was it to divide the property as it was done in that will?"

"Mr. McHenry's. In such a matter, my obligation is to carry out the wishes of the client."

"Did you in any way advise or caution him about potential problems with such an arrangement?"

"Certainly. I would have been remiss in my duties had I not pointed out to him that such an unequal disposition of the estate could cause hard feelings among the children and increase the possibility of legal action down the road."

"And what was his response to that?"

"He pretty much dismissed the concerns. He said he wanted to leave the ranch in the son's hands because he felt that running a ranch was a job for a man. He also said he thought his children were sensible enough not to resent the arrangement and that his daughter would probably be married and living with her husband in any event."

"I want to be very clear on this point, Mr. Marchand. Would it be fair to say that Frank McHenry felt strongly enough about leaving the ranch to his son to insist upon it, even after you had pointed out the potential difficulties with that disposition of the estate?"

"At that time, yes."

Bosso paused for effect, wrinkling his brow as though carefully thinking through his next set of questions. "All right," he continued, "Let's move ahead to the second will. When was that drawn up and signed?"

"In the summer of 1988."

"And was there any particular reason for doing it then?"

"There was. Mr. McHenry's wife, Elizabeth, had died in 1984, and I had been gently urging him since that time to revise his will."

"Why did it take him four years to do it?"

"I'm sure you're aware, counselor, that a great many people postpone doing their wills. He just kept putting it off, and then one day he was ready to do it."

"Again, in general terms, how did this second will dispose of the bulk of the estate?"

"With his wife deceased, Mr. McHenry disposed of the ranch and its assets among the two children as he had in the previous will."

"So he once again left the ranch, the cattle and the lease holds to the son with provisions for income to the daughter?"

"That is correct."

"And did you, on this occasion, again advise him of potential difficulties with this arrangement?"

"I did. If anything, I made the point more strenuously than before."

"And how did Mr. McHenry respond?"

"Much the same way. I think he really hoped his son would take over the ranch, and he insisted on disposing of the estate on the presumption that such a thing would happen."

"To be absolutely clear about this point, then, on two separate occasions, Frank McHenry, overriding your concerns, commissioned and signed a will that, in the end, called for his son, Daniel, to inherit the ranch and its assets. Is that a fair and accurate statement?"

"I would say so, yes."

"Now can we move forward to the morning of March 29th of this year. Do you remember that day?"

"Quite vividly."

"Please describe the events of that morning as they related to the McHenry family."

"Well, shortly after nine o'clock that morning I received a phone call asking me to come to Summit County Hospital because Mr. McHenry wanted to have a new will drawn up."

"Was it Mr. McHenry who called?"

"No, sir."

"Then who placed the call to you?"

"His daughter, Ellen McHenry."

"Didn't you think that was unusual?"

"No."

Bosso raised his eyebrows dramatically and his voice imperceptibly for maximum effect.

"You didn't? Mr. Marchand, how many times in your legal career has someone other than the testator initiated the redrawing of a will?"

"I can't recall any other occasion."

"So you are telling the court that although something occurred which had never happened to you in a professional career spanning more than three decades, you did not consider that to be unusual?"

"I guess not at the time."

"Why not, Mr. Marchand?"

"You had to consider the circumstances," he said with a touch of asperity. "I knew that Frank McHenry had fallen from a horse three days earlier, broken a number of bones, and had lain in the snow for almost four hours before being discovered. Possessing that knowledge, it did not seem unusual to me that he might choose to conserve his energy by having someone else make a phone call on his behalf."

"Even though that someone else stood to benefit from the change in the will?"

"I had no way of knowing that at the time."

"But you did know that Miss McHenry was a beneficiary of all earlier wills?"

"I suppose so."

"You *suppose* so? Very well then, Mr. Marchand. And I suppose that if your clients are satisfied with that sort of sketchy knowledge of their business, it's no concern of mine. Let us proceed. After receiving the phone call from Miss McHenry, what did you do?"

"Since the matter appeared to be urgent, I canceled my morning appointments and drove straight to the hospital."

"And will you please describe what you saw when you reached Mr. McHenry's hospital room."

"Mr. McHenry was lying in his bed, on his back. His daughter was sitting in a chair to his right from my point of view and holding his left hand in hers. One of the nurses was putting away a washcloth and bowl and left within a minute of my entrance."

"Did Mr. McHenry look like his usual self?"

"No one would after what he'd been through. Physically he looked haggard and aged considerably since I had last seen him two weeks earlier. His mental faculties, however, were most acute and he was quite lucid as he spoke, if that's what you're driving at."

"Did either of the McHenrys say anything to you when you came in?"

"I believe Miss McHenry thanked me for coming."

"Is that all?"

"I'm not sure what you mean."

"Didn't Miss McHenry say something along the order of 'Thank you for getting here so fast, Howard. We — and I emphasize the word even though I am certain she did not — We need to get this taken care of quickly?'"

"She might have. I don't recall."

"So you can't rule out the possibility?"

"Not completely. I wasn't paying much attention to her greeting because I was concerned with the business at hand."

"Very well. When you got to the business at hand, did you ask Miss McHenry to leave the room?"

"No, sir, I did not."

"You didn't?" Bosso moved up to the witness stand and leaned over. In a soft, insinuating voice, he said, "Tell me, Mr. Marchand, is it customary in these parts for the primary beneficiary of a will to be present while the testator is giving instructions to his attorney?"

Gordon winced at the sledgehammer blow. Ellen turned to whisper something to her attorney, and Gordon caught just a glimpse of her profile before she turned her eyes upon the witness again.

The witness recovered quickly. "I have been in numerous conferences where husbands and wives made out wills in each other's favor and both parties were present at the same time," he said.

"That was a clever answer, Mr. Marchand, but let me rephrase the question. On how many other occasions have you redrawn a will to change the primary beneficiary and have the new primary beneficiary be present?"

"I don't believe I ever have."

"And as an experienced estate attorney, did it not occur to you that the physical presence of the primary beneficiary as the testator was giving instructions for the new will might suggest the exertion of undue influence by that party?"

"Objection, your honor." The soft tenor voice of the defense counselor interrupted the examination as he stood. He was tall, slender, pale, and fortyish with thinning brownish-gray hair and large round eyeglasses. Looking from the defense attorney to Bosso, Gordon was glad, for Ellen's sake, that the case was being heard by a judge rather than a jury.

"The question is extremely leading," he said.

"Your honor," said Bosso, "undue influence is the basis for our challenge to this will. If we can't raise the issue during examination, how can we possibly prove the facts of the case?"

For the first time since Gordon had entered the courtroom, Judge Herbert Hawkins moved. From a reclining position in his chair, he leaned forward. He looked like central casting's idea of a judge: middle-aged, gray haired, bespectacled and otherwise featureless. His voice, when he spoke, had a rasping, slightly whiny quality.

"I'll allow some latitude, counselor," the judge said. "The question of undue influence can no more be separated from this witness than wetness can be separated from water. The objection is overruled, but keep your follow-up questions to the point."

"To begin with," said Marchand, "I don't know that I would describe myself as an experienced estate attorney. I practice all kinds of law, and in a typical year I probably do as many drunk driving defenses as wills. Because of that, I perhaps was not as aware as I should have been about the appearance of impropriety. All I saw was a devoted daughter comforting her seriously injured — and, as it turned out, dying — father."

"And you never once thought that this devotion might have something to do with the terms of the new will?"

"Objection!" The defense attorney's voice took on a passion and urgency it lacked the last time around. "Your honor, that's an unfounded insinuation with no basis in the evidence introduced thus far."

"Mr. Watkins has a point, Mr. Bosso," the judge said, gesturing with his head toward the defense attorney. "You are not playing to a jury, so I'll sustain the objection and disregard the question."

"My apologies, your honor. Let's move on to the substance of the new will. Mr. Marchand, how did Mr. McHenry breach the subject, or did Miss McHenry do it for him?"

"He did it himself," said the witness testily. "Right after the nurse left, he said something to the effect of 'Howard, I've got to change the will. I don't think Dan will ever come back to the ranch, and I'm afraid of what he might do if he did. Ellen knows how to run it and I want to leave it to her.'"

"Did he say, specifically, what he was afraid of?"

"No, he didn't. I interpreted it as a statement of general concern."

"I don't think the court is interested in your interpretations, Mr. Marchand. Now when Mr. McHenry said he wanted to leave the ranch and its assets to his daughter instead of his son, were you surprised?"

"I was, a bit."

"Why was that?"

"I did think he might redress the previous inequality by dividing the property equally among the two children, but I hadn't expected him to go so far as to leave virtually everything to Miss McHenry."

"Did you say anything to him about that?"

"Yes. I essentially repeated the point I had raised with the two prior wills, pointing out the bad feelings such a division would cause and emphasizing even more strongly than before the possibility of this new document being challenged."

"How did he respond?"

"He asked me if I had any doubts about the soundness of his mind. When I replied that I hadn't, he said 'Then he hasn't got a case if he sues, so let him try. He has his own life now, and we're not a part of it any more.'"

"I will ask you again, Mr. Marchand, did you not then, considering the severity of the change in the will, entertain the possibility that Mr. McHenry might have been unduly influenced in this matter by his daughter?"

"No, I didn't. Frank McHenry was not a man who could be pushed around by anybody."

"That may have been true when he was in vigorous health, but you yourself testified that he seemed to have aged visibly in just a few days after the accident. Did it never occur to you that lying there, probably knowing he was dying, his emotional state might be as fragile as his physical condition?"

"Not at all."

"Your lack of cynicism is a refreshing antidote to the world we live in, Mr. Marchand. How large an estate are we talking about, precisely?"

"It was substantial."

"Could you be more specific?"

"As I said previously, the bulk of the estate consisted of land and cattle. Twin Creek Ranch itself consists of nearly 5,000 acres, along with a primary dwelling house, several additional dwellings for employees and guests, and numerous outbuildings. Additionally, Twin Creek Cattle Company maintained lease holds on some 9,000 acres of federal land in several locations in this county."

"How long were the leases?"

"They were 50-year leases executed at various times from 1969 to 1981, so the end dates vary accordingly."

"So they all had at least a quarter of a century remaining before they expired?

"Yes, sir."

"And how many head of cattle did the ranch possess at the time of Mr. McHenry's death."

"You obviously are not familiar with the cattle business, Mr. Bosso."

"I freely concede as much."

"Asking a cattleman how many head of cattle he owns is tantamount to asking how much money he has in his bank account. It just isn't done, and the estate asked the court to seal that information."

"Which it did. Very well, Mr. Marchand, there nevertheless was an appraisal conducted on the estate. Could you please tell us at what figure it was valued."

"The appraiser had some difficulty coming up with exact figures, owing to the nature of the estate. Five thousand acres of land, much of which is high-quality cattle pasture, is clearly valuable, but there are few recent transactions to base a comparison upon. The same is true for the leaseholds, and of course the value of the cattle themselves changes almost daily."

"Nevertheless, the appraiser did hazard a ballpark figure?"

"She did."

"And what did that come to?"

"The best estimate of assets for the estate was between eleven and fourteen million dollars, based on current knowledge of those assets."

"What do you mean, based on current knowledge?"

"Based on what we know of the estate. For instance, there might be mineral reserves beneath the property that would greatly add to its value. That would be unlikely, but after all gold and silver have been found in this county in the past. In fact, there is an abandoned mine on the ranch."

"And what were the liabilities of the estate?"

"Those were easier to calculate precisely. They came to four million, one hundred eight thousand dollars, which consisted mostly of bank debt, along with a few outstanding expenses."

"So Mr. Marchand, we are talking about a net inheritance of seven to ten million dollars. In your experience of the world, sir, have you ever known people to lie, cheat, or cut corners when that much was at stake?"

"Objection!" Watkins was on his feet. "That's another speculative and insinuating question, your honor. Counsel has introduced no evidence as yet to indicate that any of those things have occurred here."

"I'll withdraw the question and take another approach," Bosso said. "Given the substantial size of the estate, which you surely must have guessed at, did it not occur to you that Mr. McHenry was being unusually impulsive in changing his will as dramatically as he did."

There was a long pause before Marchand answered. "Impulsive, perhaps, but I wouldn't say unusually impulsive. Mr. McHenry was a man who was what he seemed to be and whose feelings were close to the skin. When he made a decision, that was that, and I accepted it as being his intention."

"Did not the dramatic reversal of fortunes in the new will, combined with Miss McHenry's clinging presence in her father's hospital room, cause you to wonder in any way what had been behind that decision?"

The pause this time was shorter, but still perceptible. "No, sir. It did not."

Bosso fixed his witness with a steely glare for a full five seconds, then let the next words out on the exhale, almost under his breath.

"The faithful family retainer." He turned from Marchand and walked back across the courtroom to his table. "No further questions."

Watkins rose to cross-examine. For ten long seconds, he looked at a sheaf of yellow legal papers spread out on the table, which he tapped nervously with a pen. Gordon couldn't help noticing the difference between his edgy, tentative behavior and Bosso's superbly controlled and theatrical performance.

"Mr. Marchand, the will that is being challenged in this court was dated March 30th, which would be a day after the conversation you just described and four days before Mr. McHenry's death. Did Mr. McHenry express any hesitation before signing the document?"

"No, sir, he did not."

"Did he read it over carefully before signing."

"Yes, he did. In fact, he questioned me on several different specific points in the document."

"Was his daughter present during the signing of the document, or during your discussions prior to that on this day?"

"No. She excused herself when I arrived and was waiting in the lobby of the hospital when I left."

"Going back to the will that was drawn in 1988, what was the status of the McHenry family at that time?"

"Frank McHenry and his daughter were both living at the ranch. She had been back from college for a couple of years and was learning the business affairs of the property. Daniel McHenry had been living and working in San Francisco ever since his graduation from college."

"And at the time of Mr. McHenry's death?"

"It was the same. Ellen was still on the ranch, and her brother was in San Francisco."

"Mr. Marchand, how long have you been doing legal work for the McHenry family?"

"More than a quarter of a century."

"And during that time, have you become fairly well-acquainted with the personalities of the family members and with the nature of their relations to each other?"

"I don't snoop into my clients' lives, if that's what you mean, but, yes, you do pick up on things."

"Mr. Bosso has made a great deal in his examination about the changes in the will and the presence of Miss McHenry at the hospital, neither of which you said unduly alarmed you. Would it be fair to state that you were probably filtering those events through your understanding of the family, and that this is why you saw nothing sinister where Mr. Bosso would have the court believe there was?"

"At some level that was probably true."

"Thank you, Mr. Marchand. I have no more questions."

Judge Hawkins leaned forward in his chair. "Mr. Bosso, it is now 3:45. How long will it take to examine your next witness?"

"Direct examination should take 30 to 45 minutes, your honor."

"We'll take a ten minute recess, then, and try to finish with the next witness today. Please be prepared in ten minutes." He banged his gavel and left the room.

Ellen stood up slowly and turned around. When she saw Gordon sitting behind her, there was a barely visible shock of recognition in her eyes, and he found himself blushing.

• • •

The first thing Gordon had noticed about Ellen McHenry was those eyes. They were blue-gray and had the unusual effect of seeming wide open and penetratingly focused at the same time. They dominated her face as though an expert had enhanced them with makeup, even though she wore none. She was not a beautiful woman by conventional standards, but she was handsome and there was something compelling about her. A few inches under six feet tall, she was slender but not frail, with wavy, auburn hair that fell just below her collar when it wasn't put up in a bun or tied in a pony tail. She had an angular nose and thin lips that framed a mouth which was sensuous when she smiled, determined when she didn't.

Their first meeting had been in early July, when Gordon had driven up from San Francisco on a Saturday in search of a place to spend a fishing holiday. It was to be more than a holiday, really. Beyond catching trout, he was hoping to get a handle on his life, and specifically to decide whether the time had come to leave the brokerage firm of Howell, Burns & Bledsoe and do something — anything — else. He thought he knew the answer, but he also knew that in order to do it, he'd have to get away and work it through. Summit County was a place he had visited several times over the years, and, through his father, he knew the sheriff, who he asked about an out-of-the way place to stay. That was how he found himself in the offices of the Twin Creek Cattle Company, located inside the main house of the McHenry ranch that summer afternoon.

"So you're looking for a place to stay and fish, Mr. Gordon?" she said. "We do have a few cabins we rent out during the summer, but we generally close them up after Labor Day." She looked at him intently, with a relaxed self-confidence. Her hair was unbound. "However, since you come with a recommendation from the sheriff, I guess we can make an exception." She turned to the computer at the left of her desk and called up a standard form.

"When would you be arriving?"

"Labor Day. Monday the 6th." She keyed it in.

"Just yourself?"

"I'll be alone Monday through Friday of the first week. My friend Sam Akers will be joining me on Saturday the 11th and staying through the second week."

"Second week?"

"Is that a problem?"

"I'm not sure. It looks like the trouble …"

"Trouble?"

"Oh, nothing that should concern you. There's a legal matter involving the ranch, and it looks as if I might be spending a fair amount of time in court then. I'm afraid I won't be a very good hostess."

Gordon shrugged. "I'm pretty self-reliant. I'll take my chances."

"Very well then." She entered the rest of the necessary information into the computer, then showed him several cabins. She had about her the simple, direct attitude of the Westerner and they were able to carry on a pleasant conversation during the tour. When it was concluded, he picked out a cabin and wrote her a deposit check. She printed out a receipt for him, and he drove off, looking very much forward to his return.

He hadn't seen much of her the first two days of his visit. On both Tuesday and Wednesday, he had gotten in some fishing in the morning, but had been forced indoors by an afternoon thunderstorm. Gordon didn't mind fishing in the rain, but he knew that an angler standing in the middle of a stream holding a nine-foot graphite rod during an electrical storm is making a strong bid for the role of lightning rod.

Wednesday afternoon the storm had begun around two in the afternoon, and the rain was coming down in sheets when he dropped into the Sportsman Bar and Grill in downtown Harperville for a beer. He was sitting unobtrusively at one end of the bar, half-listening to two men carrying on a conversation at the other end, when the word "McHenry" caused him to sit up and take notice. From what they subsequently said, Gordon was able to infer that Ellen McHenry and her brother were involved in a dispute over their father's will. Subsequent pumping of the bartender elicited the information that the trial was the subject of intense local interest and that public sentiment generally lay with Ellen.

The rain stopped at four o'clock, and Gordon drove back to the ranch, figuring on doing some reading. When he turned on the switch as he entered the cabin, two of the three bulbs in the overhead light fixture blew out. He unscrewed them and carried them up to the main house, but no one was in, so he idled about, rearranging his fishing gear, until he saw Ellen McHenry's pickup truck pull up to the house just before five-thirty.

Bulbs in hand, he walked toward the house and arrived at the front steps just as she did. Her lips were clenched together grimly, and she looked as if she were fighting back tears. Before he could react, she pulled herself together and addressed him.

"Oh, Mr. Gordon. Did the bulbs burn out? That seems to happen a lot in number three. Let me get you some replacements."

"Thank you." He paused, then decided to plunge ahead. "Since it's that time of day, could I offer you a glass of wine?"

Her head jerked slightly and she looked at him for several seconds. "That would be very nice, Mr. Gordon. Yes, I would *love* a glass of wine."

"You can drop the mister and just call me Gordon. All my friends do."

They drank the wine — an excellent Napa Valley Chardonnay with hints of oak and pear — at a picnic table near Gordon's cabin. It was overcast and pleasantly cool, and the rain had brought up a rich aroma of pine needles and sagebrush. Behind them, the main creek through the ranch babbled in the background, and an occasional sound of distant thunder punctuated their conversation. It was an atmosphere in which all senses seemed heightened.

"I don't usually ask guests what they do for a living because it's bad business," Ellen said after a sip of wine, "but are you by any chance an attorney"

"Afraid not," Gordon said, "but I plead guilty to having one in my family. My father is a judge."

"Then I can't go on about how stupid the law can be."

"Go ahead. Half the time my father would be the first to agree. Look, I couldn't help noticing that you were upset a few minutes ago. If talking would make you feel better, I promise to be discreet."

"Discreet. That's one of those words, like honor, that you never hear these days. I appreciate that, but the whole town knows anyway. Family arguments are hell, but there has to be a special section of hell reserved for family arguments that end up in court."

Gordon nodded his agreement. She filled him in on the bare facts of the matter, which he had learned at the Sportsman earlier in the day, then shook her head.

"From my own standpoint, I can accept the possibility of losing, but I can't bear the thought that this ranch, which my father built from nothing, would go where he didn't want it to. You see, Gordon, my brother has fallen in with a bad crowd and I don't like to think what they have in mind."

Gordon wondered what constituted a bad crowd in Harperville, but before he could respond, she finished her glass of wine, reached out and touched him on the arm.

"This was very nice of you, and I feel better already." She got up to leave. "But I have work to do, and I don't want to bore you."

"I'm anything but bored."

"And remember. Discreet's the word." With that, she turned and walked back to the ranch house.

• • •

The judge returned and the next witness was sworn. She was a woman in her early forties of medium height and average weight, with black hair streaked with gray. She wore blue jeans, athletic shoes, a well-pressed and starched blue blouse, and a large pair of glasses through which her eyes squinted slightly. She gave her name as Nancy Davidson, and before rising to question her, Bosso made a theatrical show of reviewing some papers, the contents of which he had undoubtedly long since committed to memory.

"Mrs. Davidson," he said, "what is your occupation?"

"I'm a nurse at Summit County Hospital." She croaked the words out and they were barely audible.

"Could you please speak a little louder, Mrs. Davidson, and remember, there's no need to be afraid. All I seek is some simple information, and I believe the judge can vouch for the fact that there is no documented evidence of my ever biting a witness."

Some chuckling rippled through the courtroom, and the witness exhaled and leaned back slightly. The Bosso magic was beginning to work its spell. He continued:

"How long have you been a nurse at the county hospital?"

"Almost seven years."

"Were you on duty at the hospital between March 26th of this year, when Mr. Frank McHenry was first brought in for treatment, and March 30th, when he signed the will?"

"I had the day shift all five days."

"And during that time, did you tend extensively to Mr. McHenry?"

"Uh huh. There weren't many patients then, and he was the worst off, so I spent more time with him than anyone else."

"Were you on duty when he was brought to the hospital following his accident?"

"Yeah. I remember because there was only an hour left on the shift when he came in, and I had to work three hours of overtime until he was settled in."

"Recognizing that you are not a physician, could I nevertheless ask you to describe his condition in general terms?"

"Well, he was in pretty bad shape. Anybody could see that. He was all banged up, and he was shaking."

"Was he conscious and capable of speech?"

"Barely. They gave him an injection of morphine right away, and after that, he'd drift in and out of consciousness, mostly out."

"Did he say anything during this time?"

"On a few occasions he'd say, 'Danny. Where's Danny?' Or, 'Get Danny. I want to see him,' things like that."

"Did you know who Danny was?"

"I knew he had a son by that name."

"In the time you were with him that night, did Mr. McHenry call for his daughter, Ellen?"

"No, but she came in a couple of hours after he was admitted."

"Were you there when she first arrived?"

"Yes. Mr. McHenry had just been wheeled out of the X-Ray unit, and I was with him in the hall, waiting for the doctor to tell me what to do next, and she walked up."

"What did he say to her?"

"He said, 'Danny. Did you get hold of Danny?'"

"And she said?"

"'I finally talked to him, Dad. He said he can't come up now, but maybe in a few days.'"

"How did Mr. McHenry take this news?"

"He didn't say anything. Just looked up at the ceiling."

"Did Miss McHenry say anything else?"

"She took his hand in hers and said, 'It's all right, Dad. I'm here. I'll see to it that everything works out.'"

"Thank you, Mrs. Davidson. Now the following morning, what time did you come to work?"

"Eight o'clock. That's when the shift starts."

"And when did you first see Frank McHenry that day?"

"About half an hour later. The first thing I did was take breakfast around to the patients, and I got to him last."

"When you entered the room that morning, was Mr. McHenry otherwise alone?"

"No. His daughter was there. She'd been there all night."

"How can you be sure of that, Mrs. Davidson?"

"I can't, I suppose, but she was wearing the same clothes as the night before, and there was a cot in the corner of the room."

"Could you describe Mr. McHenry's physical condition that morning."

"He didn't look too good. His skin was pale and his breathing was loud and labored. Sometimes at the end of a breath, he'd let out a little whimper, sort of. He was lying on his back looking at the ceiling, and his eyes had that wide open look of fear in them. I've seen that in a lot of people who knew they were dying."

"Would it be fair to characterize his physical condition at that time as fragile?"

"I think — yes, I think so."

"As he was lying there, then, in a fragile physical condition, was there any conversation going on between him and his daughter?"

"When I started in the door, I could hear her saying, 'There's still time to do something, dad. You have to make up your mind."

"Was there any response?"

"He just lay there breathing and looking at the ceiling. Then he said, 'I don't know, honey. Please don't push me. I just can't think right now.'"

"'Please don't push me?' Were those his exact words?"

"The exact words."

"Then what happened"

"She saw me coming in and put on a big smile and said, 'Oh, hi. Glad to see you. I don't think Dad's very hungry right now, but he could use some more water.'"

"Was there any further conversation while you were in the room?"

"Not really. She just kept holding his hand and saying, 'It's all right. I'm here for you. It's all right.'"

"Based on your observation, how would you characterize Miss McHenry's behavior and attitude on this occasion?"

"Well, she seemed very intent and agitated ..."

"Would it be fair to say that she seemed to be highly focused on her father, almost to the exclusion of everything else in the room?"

"Well, *I* certainly got that impression."

"Moving ahead to Sunday the 28th, did you see Mr. McHenry and his daughter together that afternoon?"

"I did."

"What time was this?"

"About four thirty, I think. We start serving dinner around four o'clock on Sunday, and Mr. McHenry's plate was usually the last one I delivered."

"Were Mr. McHenry and his daughter talking when you entered the room?"

"She was. She was saying, 'Think about the future of the ranch, Dad. All I have to do is call Howard in the morning, and he'll take care of it.'"

"And did her father respond?"

"He just lay there for the longest time, and finally he said, 'I guess you're right, El. Oh, God, why has it come to this? You probably know better than I do right now.'"

"Were those his exact words, Mrs. Davidson — 'You probably know better than I do right now?'"

"They were. I'll never forget them."

"Then what?"

"Well, Miss McHenry put her head down next to her father's and gave it a little hug. Then she said, 'You're doing the right thing, dad. You'll be a new man when this is taken care of.'"

"Did either Mister or Miss McHenry notice your presence at the time?"

"Not a clue. I had to cough and rattle the tray a bit to get their attention. She looked up then and didn't even bother putting on her smile. Just said, 'Dinner's here, dad. See if you can eat a little more now. You have to be ready to face Howard in the morning.'"

"Mrs. Davidson, you have stated that you were on duty at the hospital the first four days Mr. McHenry was in the hospital. During that time, on how many occasions did you have an opportunity to see him and his daughter together?"

"I couldn't say exactly. It was several times a day."

"And on all those occasions, can you remember a single instance in which Mr. McHenry's behavior could have been characterized as energetic?"

"I'm afraid not."

"Can you recall a single instance when you saw the two together and Miss McHenry was not — by a decisive margin — doing most of the talking?"

"No."

"Would it be fair to say that on every occasion on which you saw the two of them together, her level of energy and intensity was substantially greater than his?"

"Yes."

"Thank you, Mrs. Davidson. That's all." Bosso turned to Watkins. "Your witness."

The defense attorney sat at his chair for a full two minutes, flipping through the notes he had been taking, nervously tapping his pen on the table all the while. When he stood, he addressed the judge and not the witness.

"Your honor," he said, "It's 4:45 now, and this is likely to be a lengthy and detailed cross-examination. In view of that, I was wondering if you might consider calling it a day and starting afresh tomorrow."

The judge gave him a long, hard look. "I appreciate what you're saying, counsel, but remember that I am obligated to hold court in the next county tomorrow. If court adjourns now, we won't be able to resume until Monday morning. Is that what you want?"

"If it would be acceptable to your honor."

"Mr. Bosso?"

Bosso looked over at Watkins, who nodded his head almost imperceptibly.

"While my client is anxious to see justice done speedily, this is agreeable under the circumstances."

"All right," said the judge. "We'll resume at ten o'clock Monday morning." He paused and looked at Watkins again. "If necessary. Court is adjourned."

Dan McHenry was the first one out of the courtroom, moving swiftly to the aisle and avoiding eye contact with his sister, who remained seated at her table until he was gone. Bosso put his papers in a briefcase with great deliberation, then began to leave. As he reached the gate to the aisle and was in a position behind Ellen McHenry, he caught Watkins' eye and raised a shoulder almost imperceptibly, as if to say, "Well?" Watkins waved him off, and the big city attorney walked briskly out of the small-town courtroom.

"How can he make it sound like that?" she asked, her husky voice shaking slightly. "I stayed with my father to the end while my brother phoned in from San Francisco, and now I'm coming across as the wicked witch who cast a spell and made him change his will."

Watkins coughed, then talked to the floor. "Well, that *is* their case, and unfortunately your family attorney didn't help you by taking the precautions he should have to preserve appearances."

"Screw appearances. I was concerned about my father."

"I know, I know." He tried to be soothing. "It just looked awkward, that's all. If it makes you feel any better, I think we got through that witness tolerably well. Bosso made some points, but I don't think he made his case."

"How bad is it?"

"It could be better. I'd give my right arm for a witness who'd testify that you and your father discussed this long before he fell off the horse."

"You don't have those discussions in front of witnesses," she said. "Except when you're in the hospital and some busybody nurse only hears snatches of the conversation out of context."

"Look, Ellen, I'm going to try to meet with Bosso tomorrow ..."

"Forget it. I'm not settling. Even if it means losing everything."

Watkins grew more assertive than he had seemed capable of doing. "I won't bill you for the time if you want, but I need to know if he's thinking settlement. The judge certainly is, and I wouldn't be doing my job if I didn't sound out the other side."

She stood up and let her breath out. "God, what a mess," she said.

"I'll call you tomorrow afternoon. Don't worry. It'll work out."

Before she could argue with him, he scooped up his attaché case and headed out the door. After a few seconds, she stood and turned around, her eye meeting Gordon's. He realized, with a start, that they were the only two people left in the courtroom, and that she must know he had overheard the conversation. He stood up as she walked down the aisle.

"So what brings you here, Gordon? Morbid curiosity?"

He looked her in the eye for a moment, and when he spoke it was in a low, measured voice with a hint of a tremor.

"I think," he said, "that 'concern' would be a more accurate characterization."

She lowered her eyes. "I'm sorry. I'm not myself now. Please forgive me."

He nodded. "I'll do more than that. I'll invite you to dinner."

"I'd like to," she said, "but not now. I need to get back to the ranch and compose myself. Thank you for asking." With that, she walked briskly away.

After giving her two minutes' head start, Gordon left the courtroom and got to the front door of the courthouse just as the janitor was beginning to lock it. He stepped outside to find that the rain had stopped falling, though it was overcast and darkening. Rain or no rain, he thought, he would be back at the courthouse Monday at ten o'clock.

Friday September 10

When Gordon drove to the East Buchanan River shortly after eight o'clock in the morning, he found, as he had feared, that it was running high and muddy, the color of coffee with cream. There would be no fishing it for a couple of days.

Being familiar with the area, however, he knew that thunderstorms hit the mountains in a patchwork pattern, and that one area might be inundated while another, only a few miles away, might receive only light rainfall. He also knew that smaller streams tended to clear up faster than the East Buchanan, which was far and away the largest body of running water in the area. The West Fork of the Buchanan (or at least the upper part of it) was one range over and substantially smaller — no more than a creek, really. The fish wouldn't be as large, but it was a beautiful stream and at this time of year there were likely to be few people around. He decided to check it out.

He drove his Cherokee back through Harperville and several miles up the state highway. It was a cool morning, with not a cloud in the sky, and even though the calendar still said summer, it felt like fall. The leaves on the aspens had not yet begun to turn gold, and a hint of a breeze made them shimmer and quiver. A feeling of contentment washed over him. Even if the West Buchanan turned out to be high and muddy, it would be worth the drive on a morning like this.

Ten minutes from Harperville, he turned left on a paved county road that more or less paralleled the West Buchanan for a couple of miles. Gordon was pleased to see that the water was clear. There would be fishing today after all. About two miles up the county road, the West Buchanan ran under it, from left to right, coming down from its source, Tamarack Lake, high in the mountains above. A half-mile beyond the bridge, a dirt road went off to the left, the same direction as the stream. Gordon made the turn, crossed a cattle guard, and began the final leg of his trip.

For five miles he followed a narrow, twisting dirt road through dense forest, interrupted by an occasional open space, until he reached Sullivan Meadows. At an elevation of seven thousand feet, the meadows were the first place the West Buchanan slowed down after leaving the source lake twenty five hundred feet higher up. The creek worked its way slowly through the grassy fields in a series of slow riffles, deep pools, and undercut banks, all home to trout. Someone — he wondered if it was the McHenrys — had a lease to graze cattle here. The stream was still on the left side of the road as he drove up, and access to it was unobstructed. Across the creek, a fence ran parallel to it with just a few feet of clearance and a couple of breaks that allowed the cows to drink from the deeper pools they couldn't wade across. There were two or three hundred head in the pasture, and they were wearing bells so they could be found if they wandered into the forest or nearby underbrush. The almost continuous sound of the bells mixed with the whisper of the pines and aspens in the breeze to put just a hint of tension in the air.

In the upper end of the meadow, there was a large flat area where the grass had been matted down or worn away and several impromptu fire pits had been formed with circles of stone. It was not an official campground, but the Forest Service allowed people to stay there as long as fire rules were obeyed.

Expecting to have the meadow to himself, Gordon was dismayed to see a large encampment in place. He counted seven substantial tents, ten pickups and sport utility vehicles, and about a dozen horses tethered near the creek. During the summer a riding club would sometimes claim the meadow for a weekend, using it as a base camp for excursions that followed the creek to the wilderness area above. He guessed that such a group must be having one last weekend outing while the weather was still good. Gordon sat in the Cherokee in the middle of the road at the bottom of the meadow, trying to decide whether to proceed with his plans or turn back.

Surveying the scene, he thought he could start fifty yards below the camp and work his way down the bottom third of the meadow, which had some prime fishing water in it, then continue through the pocket water in the wooded section below. Since the group seemed to be sticking to its camp, he figured that he ought to enjoy a fair degree of solitude.

Gordon pulled a few feet off the road and began dressing to fish. Sitting on the back flap of his vehicle, he put on a pair of hip waders and pulled the wading boots over them. He looked at the nine-foot graphite rod he had rigged to fish the East Buchanan and decided against it, reaching instead for a seven and a half foot, five-weight bamboo rod that was a favorite of his. Taking it out of its case, he joined the two halves together, screwed the reel on to it and ran the line through the ferrules. He put on his fishing vest, then removed a seven-and-a-half-foot 5X leader from it, attached it to the line, tied on a size 14 Yellow Humpy, bent back its barb with pliers and slipped the hook into the small ring just above the handle. He was ready to go.

It was a quarter past nine as Gordon strolled down a slight grade into the heart of the meadow. The sun had risen high enough above the mountains to bathe almost the entire meadow in its light and begin warming it up. The grass was still wet from the morning dew, and it quickly covered his boots and waders with a film of water. He made his way toward a pool, below the encampment, where he reasoned there might be some fish if this group hadn't worked the water to death.

About 25 feet from the creek, he got down on his knees and took stock. The stream was fairly full for late season and the pool seemed to be about six feet deep. He decided to try a few casts that would bring his fly from the riffle above to the head of it, then, if that drew no response, try drifting his fly down the tail end of the pool, where a trout or two might be waiting.

He crept a little closer, freed the fly and stripped some line from the reel. His first cast hit the riffle about five feet above the pool and drifted cleanly down to the quiet water. It glided five or six feet into the pool, then stalled in the still water. Gordon sat watching it for nearly a minute, then shook his head. He repeated the cast three more times with the same result, then decided to try the bottom half of the pool. He moved to the head of it and closer to the water. Facing downstream, his back to the encampment, he sized up the situation. Some brush overhung the tail end of the pool on the opposite shore and there might be fish taking cover beneath it. After a couple of back casts, he aimed for a spot 17 feet downstream at the edge of the brush. He hit the target with a flawless cast and intently watched the fly drift lazily downstream.

"Catching anything?"

The question was asked at the precise instant that a trout rose to take the fly, and it so startled Gordon that he involuntarily jerked the rod and pulled the fly from the fish's mouth. It landed in the middle of the pool and sat motionless.

"Sorry about that. I hate to cost a man a fish."

The words were spoken by a man who stood six-feet two and was powerfully built. He was in his late twenties and wore his black hair in a crew cut. His mouth was set in a smile that bordered on a sneer, and the tone of his voice, which carried a hint too much of honeyed unctuousness, belied his words. He had a toothpick in his mouth and was fixing Gordon with an unflinching stare. After the start the man had given him, Gordon found the gaze unnerving.

"That's all right," he said without conviction. "I didn't hear you coming."

"I'm surprised you got a rise. This creek got pretty well fished out over Labor Day and they haven't stocked it since. You might be better off trying the East Buchanan." The last words came out in a way that made them sound more like a threat than friendly advice.

Gordon chose to be deliberately obtuse. "I checked that out this morning, and it's muddy from all the rain.

Besides, this is a nice creek, and I'm sure there are still some fish in the pocket water below the meadow."

"Have it your way," said the man. "It's still a free country." He paused momentarily. "It's none of my business again, but you did say you were going to fish downstream a bit?"

Gordon nodded.

"Just a word of caution. There are a lot of rattlesnakes on the rocks downstream, so you might want to watch your step. In fact, the snakes are better sport than the fish. I like to go after them with a stick and a loop myself. I got four the day before yesterday." He paused and smiled. "One of them was fifty three inches long."

He made no attempt to leave, letting that last nugget of information sink in, so Gordon felt compelled to say something.

"Are you folks from a horseman's association or something?'

"No, not really. You might say we're sort of a gun club. As a matter of fact, I was coming down here to tell you that we're about ready to start a little target practice. I hope the noise won't bother you."

Gordon shrugged. "It's still a free country," he said.

"Right you are." The man stayed put, looking at Gordon, who nervously reeled in the fly and hooked it to the rod handle.

"I think I'll work my way downstream," Gordon said. "Nice meeting you."

"By the way," said the stranger, "and I know this is none of my business, but is that the way you usually dress when you're fishing?"

Gordon was wearing khaki pants, a forest-green flannel shirt, tan fishing vest and brown Stetson. "Is there some problem?"

"No, I wouldn't exactly call it a problem. It's just that, you see, deer hunting season starts tomorrow and right now you're about the same color as a deer. If you go tramping through the brush in that outfit, somebody might take a shot at you." He paused. "I'd really hate to see that happen."

"So would I," said Gordon. "Thanks for the advice."

"Well, good luck. Hope you catch something today."

He walked off leaving Gordon feeling rattled. The man had never raised his voice, but if his intent was to convey a sense of menace, he had certainly succeeded.

Gordon decided to put some more distance between himself and the encampment and started downstream. The sound of the bells from the cattle had taken on an ominous tone and frequency, almost as if the animals themselves were sharing his uneasiness and moving more nervously. He reached a bend in the creek, about 150 feet below the spot where the conversation had been held, and decided to cast to the undercut bank on the other side.

The fly hit the water two feet from the opposite bank. Too far, Gordon thought, as he watched it drift. The sun was hitting the water directly by now, and he could easily follow the tan-colored fly on the surface. He tried again, and this time got it just six inches out from the bank. A split second later, it was hammered by a scrappy ten-inch trout. Playing the fish quickly and deftly, Gordon brought it to his shore and stabilized it in the water with his left hand. He rarely used a net because he felt it was easier on the fish to keep it in the water. This one was a brook trout, and judging from its deep colors, a native. Sliding his right hand down the end of the leader, he grasped the hook between thumb and forefinger. It was firmly lodged in the right corner of the fish's lower lip, but with an expert twist, Gordon had it out. He then took his left hand away from the fish, which swam off immediately to the cover of the overhanging bank on the other side.

"Not bad for a fished-out creek," he muttered under his breath.

He heard the first shot as he attempted another cast. It was quickly followed by two more, then a series of perhaps half a dozen in quick succession. The sound bounced off the sides of the surrounding mountains and filled the meadow. The firing continued, shots coming nearly every other second, for a full three minutes before there was a pause. It was a deep, reverberating sound, much like the thunder of the previous afternoon, only louder. When the gunfire stopped, there was some whooping and shouting from the direction of the encampment, and Gordon figured the men must be checking the bullet holes in the targets and adding up points. Then, a moment later, the shooting started again.

Although he disliked guns, Gordon did his best not to be bothered by the shooting. He moved slightly downstream and tried casting to another section of undercut bank. His first effort was a foot too long, and his fly snagged in a piece of brush on the other side. He tried pulling on the line and succeeded only in breaking off his fly. Squatting on the ground to tie on a new one, he was acutely aware of the discordant symphony of cowbells and gunfire. When he tried another cast, he snagged his fly in the same overhanging brush as before.

Gordon swore. It was no use. The visit from the stranger and the sound of the gunfire had shaken him and he had no inclination to stay any longer. He walked back to his car and when he got there looked back at the encampment. About a hundred feet from the edge of camp, in the direction opposite from where he had been fishing, he could see five large targets set up against a background of stacked hay. Five men with rifles were shooting at them from the edge of camp. One of them was the man who had come to talk with Gordon, and after firing off a few rounds, he turned and looked in the direction of Gordon's vehicle. He waved, and Gordon waved back.

But Gordon was hardly looking at the stranger. He was more interested in the targets themselves. They were life-sized human silhouettes, topped with cut-out pictures of the faces of Bill and Hillary Clinton.

• • •

Contacts. One of the things about being the son of a judge was that Gordon had contacts. Twelve years ago, his father had spent July and August as a visiting judge in Summit County when the local jurist had been sidelined with appendicitis. It was the summer after Gordon had graduated from Berkeley, and he had spent those two months with his father, living in a rented cabin and fishing nearly every day. With a degree in hand and a job lined up at the brokerage, Gordon for the first time felt that he had reached adulthood, and he and his father had enjoyed each other's company during that time. He came to know the area well and developed an affinity for it that had brought him back several times since.

He and his father had made some acquaintances at the time, and one of them was Sheriff Mike Baca. The sheriff was something of a legend in Summit County, having been under 30 years of age when he first won the office. He was now nearing the end of his sixth four-year term and hadn't run in a contested election since being convincingly re-elected to his second term. There had been three murders in the county while Baca was sheriff, and in each case the investigation had resulted in an arrest and conviction. His detailed knowledge of his territory made his search and rescue team one of the best in the state, and almost every summer, Gordon would see a story in the *San Francisco Chronicle* about its finding some lost child or hiker.

After giving up on fishing the West Buchanan, Gordon decided to presume on his acquaintance and pay the sheriff a call. He usually did when he was in the area, and he knew Baca could probably tell him plenty about both the McHenry family and the encampment on the West Buchanan. It was a little past 11 o'clock when Gordon parked in front of the courthouse, entered the front door, and went down the steps to the sheriff's basement office. The receptionist recognized him as he walked in the door.

"Quill Gordon! I thought I saw you heading up to the second floor yesterday afternoon."

"You probably did, Ginger. Is the sheriff in?"

"He sure is. How long are you here for?"

"I'll be around till the end of next week. Is he still in the same office?"

"Yup. Just go back and knock."

Gordon went through a swinging door, walked past the receptionist and three other desks, two of them vacant, to a door with a frosted-glass window. He rapped on the glass, then went in when bid to do so. The sheriff was looking raptly at a large color computer screen, but when he saw who his visitor was, he stood, and extended his hand.

"What took you so long to come by? You've been up here since Monday."

"How did you know that?"

"It's my job to know what's going on. I can tell you where you've been fishing every day, and if you weren't on vacation I'd warn you against drinking beer in saloons in the middle of the afternoon. It's driven a lot of men to ruin. Have a seat."

Gordon sat down and took a good look at Baca. He was a large man, standing six-four, with a stocky frame. His hair was just perceptibly grayer than when Gordon last saw him two years ago and was a bit thinner on top, and the mustache was almost completely gray now. He wore khaki uniform pants and a matching short-sleeve shirt with an open collar that revealed a white undershirt beneath and left his heavily tanned arms exposed. His solid features were accented by the aviator glasses he wore, and his trademark white Stetson lay on the desk at his side.

"Am I catching you at a bad time?" Gordon asked. "You were looking at that computer pretty seriously."

"If the truth be known, I was going through yesterday's box scores on Compuserve. It's amazing what you can do with a computer these days."

"That one looks brand new."

"Law enforcement has to keep up with the times," Baca said a bit defensively. "This is how we handle information now."

"Well, if you're looking up the box scores, business must be slow."

"Except for one thing, it's been blessedly slow since Labor Day. How are things with you?"

"Pretty good." Gordon paused. "I was hoping you could fill me in on a little local color."

"What's on your mind?"

"Well, yesterday afternoon, when the thunderstorm chased me off the river, I stopped by the courthouse and watched a little of the action in Superior court."

Baca raised his eyebrows slightly. "Interesting, wasn't it?"

"Very. I gather that it's quite the talk of the town. I was wondering if you could give me a little background."

"It's a sad story, really," Baca said. "Frank McHenry had one of the most beautiful cattle ranches in the state of California, put it together piece by piece starting just after the war. He was an older man when he married, and from the day his boy was born he dreamed of passing it on to the son. But as time went on, it didn't look like it was going to work out. I don't know how much you've heard, but as things turned out," he paused, "Dan McHenry was queer."

"So that's the unspoken element," said Gordon. "But he could still run the ranch."

"Doesn't want to. Or maybe I should say didn't until the last year or so. He's been living his own life in San Francisco pretty much since he went off to college."

"When did the family find out?"

"He told them about five years ago. He waited until his mother had died, which was kind. I think they had an idea before that, and I'm sure Ellen knew. I will say that Frank took it pretty well. He was a devout Catholic and a very conservative man, but he accepted his son for what he was."

"Frank McHenry never remarried?"

Baca smiled. "That was one of the town's most interesting little stories. A couple of years after his wife died, Frank took up with Kitty Stevens who owns Mom's Cafe."

"Oh, sure. I'm one of her best customers."

"Anyway, they were pretty seriously involved, but since she was divorced, Frank wouldn't marry her. Contrary to church doctrine and all that. But they did everything together, and she became like a second mother to Ellen. He left her a handsome bequest in his will to put her daughter through college, and it should do that all right."

"Well, this makes things a little more clear. I take it, then, that the gay scene in San Francisco is what his sister meant when she said he'd fallen in with a bad crowd."

"Oh no no. That's the rest of the story." Baca leaned forward across the desk. "Does the name Rex Radio mean anything to you?"

Gordon whistled. "The talk show host Rex Radio? The one who got fired for making hate remarks on the air?"

"The same. You might also remember that one of his running themes was that people should form their own posses for self-protection and take the police power away from the state. Well, apparently he's been acting on his own advice and putting together a highly armed group of his own. Dan McHenry got drawn into that crowd."

"This gets stranger by the minute," Gordon said. "How do you suppose that happened?"

"With something like that, it's hard to say. He grew up here, where almost everybody's white, so he never had much exposure to minorities. In his first quarter in college, he was in San Francisco one night and got mugged and beaten up badly by several black kids. Even as a kid, he always remembered an insult, and the family thinks he may have nursed his grievance over the mugging until it consumed him."

"Too bad."

"Then when he was up here a year ago he made a real scene at a barbecue at the ranch. He'd had a few drinks, but that's no excuse for the language he was using. He said we had to arm ourselves against the quote —niggers and Mexicans — unquote or they'd murder us in our beds. And he came up to me and told me that I was illegally in possession of police power as an agent of the government and that a people's posse would be taking over for me soon."

"What did you do?"

"I asked him if he or anybody in his so-called people's posse had ever gone before the voters and won an election. He didn't appreciate that and stomped off. But I don't mind telling you I was upset. I don't like hate and anger, and there was a lot of it in his talk."

"So you think that's why Frank McHenry disinherited his son."

"No doubt in my mind. He was a tightfisted, stubborn, conservative old man, but he wasn't a hater. I really think that's what did it."

"This is fascinating. But why would a group like that take in a gay man? You'd think that would be high on the list of things they dislike."

Baca laughed. "They'd sign up a Democrat if they thought it would give them a shot at controlling something like the McHenry ranch. You see, a base of operations would be really valuable to a crowd like that. A place where they could keep a lot of men and weapons and practice whatever sorts of war games it is they practice. I suspect that's why Dan McHenry and his boyfriend, a fellow name of George, are part of that budding posse, and I think Frank McHenry and his daughter were just beginning to realize where it was all going when Frank had his fall."

"So there's more to this than a dispute between brother and sister."

"A lot more. Rex Radio hired that San Francisco lawyer to challenge the will, and from the look of things, he might succeed. He and his entourage have taken over

Sullivan Meadows on the West Buchanan and are waiting out the verdict there."

"That explains it," Gordon said. He told the sheriff about his trip to the meadow that morning and the reception he had received from the representative of the encampment.

"Doesn't surprise me," said Baca. "They've scared off just about everybody who goes up there, and the way they do it is all perfectly legal. A veiled threat or two, then when they start their quote unquote target practice, not many people want to stick around."

"Do you have any idea who I was talking to?"

"From your description, I'd guess Hart Lee Bowen. He was an all-conference linebacker at Arizona State a few years ago, and now he's Rex Radio's personal bodyguard."

"You must be staying on top of that group."

Baca turned to the computer at the side of his desk. "Do you remember I said business was slow except for one thing? That one thing is Mr. Radio and his friends. As soon as I get in every morning, again after lunch, and again at the end of the day, I check the e-mail in this baby. I'm sending almost daily reports to an FBI agent who's been tracking the Posse Comitatus for the last five years. And there's an agent named Bill Boyd at the Bureau of Alcohol, Tobacco and Firearms who wants to know how many guns those people are moving. Almost every time I look in the computer, there's something here from one or both of them."

"So you're playing cat and mouse until the trial's over?" Baca nodded. "Do you think Dan McHenry can win?"

"He's got the better lawyer," said the sheriff, "and that always helps. Bosso got Judge Courtney disqualified and Judge Hawkins from Fresno to hear the case. And from what I understand, Ellen McHenry said and did some things when the old man was dying that don't look too good now."

"Do you think she did anything wrong?"

"Me? No, only from the sake of appearances. But it's how it appears to the judge that matters."

"She seems like a strong woman."

"Oh, she knows her mind, all right. And she's doing a bang-up job of running that ranch. Speaking of which, what time did you leave there this morning?"

"About seven o' clock. Why?"

"Then this will be news to you. At seven thirty, Ellen McHenry went into the main barn to feed the horses. When she pushed the barn door open, a sixty pound bale of hay that had been balanced on top of it fell down and missed her by an inch."

"Good God!"

"She was lucky. She had to push the door harder because of the weight of the hay, and she ended up moving off to her right just a bit. If the door had opened in the usual way, the hay would have hit her on the head. She could have been killed."

"Could it have been an accident?"

"Not unless bales of hay have learned to walk across a barn and elevate themselves to the top of a twelve-foot door. And I'll tell you something else. There's not much doubt it was aimed at her. Anybody who knows the routine of the ranch could tell you that she goes into that barn every morning to feed the horses and that she's almost always the first one through that door."

"Who ..." Gordon was unable to finish the question.

"I think you'll find the answer to that in Sullivan Meadows. I can't prove it, of course, but it looks to me that someone is impatient with the speed at which the wheels of justice move and decided to bring matters to a conclusion here and now."

The two men sat for a moment in silence, which Gordon finally broke. "I'm just wondering. Suppose the challenge to the will succeeds ..."

"Or there's another 'accident.'"

"Or there's another accident and that crowd takes over the ranch. Once they have it, what are they going to do next?"

Baca smiled. "Well, I'm up for re-election next year. I expect I'd be their first target."

• • •

After lunch, Gordon drove back to the ranch to check on Ellen McHenry. He knocked on the door of the ranch house and was surprised when Kitty Stevens opened it.

"I'm sorry. I was looking for Ellen."

"Gordon, right?"

"Yes. I just heard about what happened this morning and I wanted to see if she's all right."

"She's all right and she's not here. Won't be back until sundown. Would you like to come in and have a beer?"

He wavered a moment, remembering Baca's temperance counsel, then said, "Sure."

Kitty vanished into the kitchen and returned a minute later with two bottles of Miller Genuine Draft. She handed one to Gordon and bade him sit down on the large couch facing the fireplace. She sat in a comfortable padded chair perpendicular to him. She was a large-boned, full-figured woman in her early fifties with tousled grey-gold hair, large eyes, large mouth and a casual, impertinent manner that lent itself to sassing back the teasing customers at her cafe. The large eyes were fixed on Gordon as she took a pull of her beer and swallowed.

"You've been taking an interest in my Ellen, Gordon. That shows good taste on your part, but I like to know something about that kind of man."

"Really," he said. "I'm a guest here, albeit a paying one, and I think it's just common decency to inquire after my hostess when she's narrowly avoided a bad accident."

"So you don't deny it. Good. Now let me see if I can tell you something about yourself. You've had breakfast at my cafe three out of the last four mornings. I've always said that you can learn more about a man from the way he eats breakfast than you can from talking to him for a month. Do you want to know what your breakfast says about you, Gordon?"

"If you eat at Mom's, that says you're well-fed."

"Thanks, but let's get back to you. You walk into the cafe in the morning, and the first thing you do is look around very carefully. Then you always pick out the table that's the most isolated. It's obvious you want to have your own space. You'd buy a box of corn flakes at the grocery store and eat them in the parking lot before you'd sit at the counter with a stranger on either side of you."

Gordon moved uneasily in the couch.

"When you get to the table, you open your newspaper or whatever you brought to read and start right in on it. You read all the way through the meal and pay no attention to what's going on around you. The fact that you're reading and are so focused about it tells me you're smart and have remarkable concentration. I suspect that serves you well in the business world."

He tilted his head downward and to the side in acknowledgement.

"You also crack a smile from time to time when you're reading, which tells me you have a sense of humor. You drink your coffee black, which is the sign of a no-nonsense man. Every morning you order scrambled eggs and hash browns, but you change the meat. Bacon Tuesday, sausage Wednesday and ham today. It's almost like you're in denial about being in a rut, so you change one thing every day. And you eat your food separately, but move back and forth between items so the portions grow smaller at the same rate. That suggests meticulousness." She paused for a second. "Frank used to do that, you know. By the way, I'm dying to know if you go back to bacon the next time or skip sequence and go for the sausage."

"Your sausage is very good. Do you mind if I ask where you get it?"

"A market in Reno that makes their own. They're very good. And finally, you tip 20 percent. That shows you're not cheap and have some sympathy for a poor working waitress." She took a long draw on her beer and looked at him with a playful smile.

After ten seconds of silence, Gordon replied, "I wonder what you could tell about me from a four-course dinner."

"We'll find out tomorrow. You're coming to the barbecue, aren't you?"

"I'm sorry."

"Of course. Ellen said she was going to invite you but hadn't gotten around to it yet. The second Saturday in September is the McHenry roundup barbecue. It's quite an event. There'll be a couple hundred people here at least. You will come, won't you."

"I'd be delighted."

"And the last thing you just showed me is that you're a gentleman. You don't see too many of those these days."

"I try." Gordon finished off his beer and stood up. "Thanks for the beer and please tell Ellen I called."

She walked him to the door. As he turned to say goodbye, she stepped close to him.

"Listen, Gordon. Ellen's going through a lot right now." She jabbed her forefinger into his chest. "She's a girl who feels things deeply and she really appreciated your talking to her the other night. But don't rush her."

He walked across the open space to his Cherokee. As he got in, he instinctively put his hand on his shirt to reassure himself after that discussion that he had not, indeed, been sitting naked in front of Kitty.

• • •

Gordon spent the rest of the afternoon driving aimlessly around the county, checking out the condition of the streams and lakes. At one or two of them he stopped and fished for a few minutes, but his heart wasn't in it. At five o'clock he drove back to Harperville and stopped at the Sportsman for a drink at the bar before repairing to the dining room.

The Sportsman (Established 1925) was a Summit County landmark. The one frosted window near the door let in a small quantity of late afternoon light, without seriously brightening the comforting gloom within. A long bar took up most of one side of the room, the left side for those entering by the front door. Across from the bar, near the opposite wall, were two pool tables and in the middle of the floor was an open space for dancing. A few tables lined the wall to the right of the entrance. The decor was simple and unpretentious. On the wooden walls, stained dark by years of accumulated tobacco smoke, hung the stuffed and mounted heads of 14 bucks with impressive antlers, along with a hodgepodge of press clippings and faded snapshots of hunters and anglers posed with their kill. About three dozen bras were tacked to the acoustical tile ceiling.

Nursing a scotch and soda, Gordon found himself in conversation with a divorced teacher, who was trying to forget about her husband and the first week of school with the help of vodka and tonic. Gordon was suspicious of vodka drinkers and tried to limit his response to general murmurs of assent to the propositions that her ex-husband was a bastard and that third-graders were becoming more ill-behaved with each passing year.

He was looking at the doorway leading to the restaurant and wondering how he could politely extricate himself when four men walked through the door. One was Bowen, the man who had accosted him at the West Buchanan that morning, and another was Dan McHenry. The third was a man in his late twenties with a delicate face, partially hidden by a neatly trimmed beard the same sandy color as his thinning hair, who clung to McHenry's side as if welded there. He was the first to speak.

"Let's get that table over there," he said, motioning to the far corner. "We can talk there."

"You go claim the table, George," Bowen said. "You're real good at that." The words were spoken softly, but Bowen's voice gave them an undertone of sarcasm that caused George to glare.

"Come on, Danny," he said.

"You go along, George," said young McHenry. "I'll be along in a couple of minutes."

George looked at his three companions then went to the table, sat down by himself, and began inspecting an ash tray ostentatiously. Meanwhile, Bowen had noticed Gordon and leaned over to say something under his breath to the fourth man. He was in his early fifties, stood six feet tall, and was a fit 175 pounds. His slick, dark hair, graying a little at the sideburns, was combed straight back, accentuating his prominent forehead. With that forehead, a sharply defined nose, and a strong chin, his face looked chiseled, rather than sculpted. He looked at the world through keen eyes set in a squint that seemed like a perpetual glare. Gordon had no trouble recognizing him from TV images and newspaper photographs as Rex Radio.

"You boys have a seat," said Radio. "I have to do a little socializing."

He strode to the bar and stood next to Gordon, on the opposite side from the schoolteacher. "Excuse me for interrupting," he said, "but if I'm not mistaken, you're the young man who was up fishing by our camp on the West Buchanan this morning." Gordon nodded. "And you," turning to the teacher, "must be his lovely wife."

She began to giggle. Radio had a deep, resonant, honeyed voice, and his ability to use it as a finely tuned instrument had been well honed over the years. He had put her — and even Gordon, to some extent — at their ease immediately.

"Could I buy you a drink?" he asked. "I'd consider it a pleasure."

Gordon didn't really want to tarry at the bar, but there was no graceful way out of the situation. Radio called for Old Crow on the rocks. "Mark Twain used to drink it," he said as an aside. "Anything that's good enough for Mark Twain is good enough for me."

When the bartender brought the drinks, Radio reached into his jeans pocket and pulled out a large roll of money that caused even Gordon, who was accustomed to carrying more cash than most, to do a double-take. He flattened out the roll on the bar, then carefully took a twenty from the top of it and held it up, as if for inspection.

"Funny thing, money," Radio said. "Nothing but paper run off a printing press in large volume. It isn't worth squat in itself, but people willingly accept it in exchange for concrete merchandise. And do you know why?" He paused. "Because it has the full faith and credit of the U.S. Government behind it. Wonder how long that'll last."

The teacher was openly staring at him, and Gordon was trying not to as he continued. "They print United States currency in twelve different cities, and every bill has a serial number on it that begins with a letter of the alphabet to tell you which city it was printed in. A is Philadelphia; B is New York, C is Boston, D is Richmond; E is Atlanta; F is Chicago; G is Minneapolis; H is St. Louis; I is Denver; J is Kansas City; K is Dallas; and L is San Francisco." He looked from the bartender to Gordon to the teacher, all of whom were listening spellbound to his monologue. "I like to keep my money in alphabetical order and spend San Francisco first." He handed the bill to the bartender. "Keep the change."

That amounted to a 100 percent tip, but when the bartender thanked him effusively, Radio cut him off.

"Don't have to thank me, son. Just spend it while it's still good." He turned to Gordon. "So how was the fishing this morning?"

"I caught one," Gordon said.

"Rainbow?"

"Brook trout."

"No fooling. I hope Hart Lee didn't upset you. He does that to people sometimes without really meaning to."

"Oh no," lied Gordon. "No problem."

"Good, good. Glad to hear it. Well, let's have a toast to the sport of fishing before the animal rights people take it away from us." He raised his bourbon and took a small sip from it. Then he set the glass on the bar and took a 6-ounce laboratory bottle from the pocket of the light jacket he was wearing and topped the drink off with water.

"Old habit of mine," he explained. "I like to drink the first swallow neat, then have the rest with water. Pure rain water. Even up here, there's no telling what kind of fluoride and crap they put in their water. But I'm changing the subject. Mind if I ask you a question?"

"You're buying. Ask away."

"I like your attitude. See, I was hoping you could settle a little wager Hart Lee and I have. He thinks you're with the FBI, but I disagree. You don't look puckered-up enough to be with the FBI."

Gordon laughed. "I guess I'll take that as a compliment. Anyway, you win. I'm just a poor stockbroker up here on a fishing trip. My name's Quill Gordon."

"Quill Gordon. Like the trout fly?" Gordon nodded. "That's why you looked familiar. You used to play basketball for Cal."

"A long time ago."

"I'm a great sports fan. What's your favorite sport, Mr. Gordon?"

"I'm still partial to basketball, I guess."

"I prefer football, myself. It's more like life than any other sport. You beat your brains out and get bloodied driving the ball upfield, then somebody fumbles and it's all for nothing. Yep. Just like life. By the way, I'm Rex Radio."

"I know," said Gordon, reluctantly shaking hands with him. "I recognized you."

"My reputation has preceded me. Let me introduce you to my friends. Boys!" The three men got up from the table and came to the bar. "Gentlemen, we're in the presence of a celebrity here, myself excluded. I'd like you to meet Quill Gordon, the best white man to play basketball for the University of California in the last 20 years."

Gordon's mouth tensed at the remark. The teacher shifted uneasily on her bar stool.

"I guess," replied Gordon coolly, "that that's a nice way of saying I wasn't very good."

"Not at all," said Dan McHenry, extending his hand. "I saw several games your senior year. I'm Dan McHenry and this is my friend George Horton."

"Delighted," said George.

"And we met this morning, though we weren't properly introduced. I'm Hart Lee Bowen."

"By the way, Hart Lee, you lose," Radio said. "Mr. Gordon here isn't with the FBI or the CIA or anybody else. He's a stockbroker in San Francisco."

"I guess you're right, Rex. He doesn't look puckered-up enough to be an FBI agent." The other three men laughed.

"I hope we can be on good terms now," Radio said. "As long as our target practice doesn't bother you."

"We take a lot of target practice," George said eagerly. His comrades gave him stern looks and he fell silent.

"Do you always practice trying to hit pictures of the Clintons?" Gordon asked.

"Not at all," said Radio. "Some days we do Martin Luther King or Cesar Chavez.

Seeing Gordon's reaction, he let loose with a loud laugh. "Don't be so politically correct, son. Nobody buys a gun these days to shoot at tin cans. The government and the bleeding heart judges don't protect us from criminals, so we have to do it ourselves. You shoot at life-size targets because you don't want the first human figure you aim at to be the one coming through your bedroom window at three in the morning."

"My father is a judge," Gordon said coolly.

"And one of the good ones, I'm sure," Radio said. "But too many of them think a weekend in jail is enough punishment for robbing a bank."

Before Gordon could answer, there was a beeping noise, and Radio pulled a cellular phone from his jacket.

"Excuse me. I've been waiting for this call. Radio here. (Pause.) He did? Good. (Pause). Fifty-fifty, huh? And what did you tell him? (Pause, then laughter) Good for you. When you got your hands around his throat, it's no time to relax. You're a warrior, Manny. I like that. (Pause) I think so. All right, then, see you Monday and have a good weekend."

He put the phone back in his jacket pocket and patted it. "Just a little legal matter I had to take care of. I don't know how we ever got along without these things."

It occurred to Gordon that the call must have been from Manfred Bosso about the McHenry trial, and he wondered why the call had gone to Radio, rather than McHenry himself.

"Did they make an offer?" Dan McHenry asked.

"More like a speculative question," Radio said, looking at Gordon. "I'll tell you about it later." He turned to Horton. "George, can you get to the store before it closes and fill up the ice chests?"

"I did it last night."

"That's right, and you did such a good job I'm asking you to do it again tonight."

"Why do I always have to be the gofer? You just think of me as your errand boy."

Radio put his hand on Horton's shoulder. "George, you're a valuable member of our team and you know that. But I expect you to do the little I ask of you and to do it without complaining." He paused and Looked Horton straight in the eye. When he spoke again, his voice had dropped an octave and acquired an ominous rumble. "Get the ice, George."

"Well, all right." He left the saloon with his head down. Gordon decided this would be a good time for him to leave as well, so he stood up.

"Thanks for the drink," he said. "It's not every day a celebrity stands a round for a stranger."

"Don't mention it," said Radio. "I'm sure we'll meet again. Oh, and let me give you a fishing tip. Some of our boys were out this afternoon and found lots of fish in Aspen Creek and Indian Creek, but where we are, the fishing's no good at all. I'd leave it alone if I were you." He smiled. "Just a little friendly advice."

Saturday September 11

Not far south of Harperville a paved road leaves the state highway and goes west into the mountains. Two miles up that road is a 40-house subdivision, half summer homes and half permanent residents. Just past the subdivision, the pavement ends and a well maintained dirt road goes over a crest and into a small valley. When the road finishes its descent into the valley, a cattle guard and a barbed-wire fence seal off Twin Creek Ranch, otherwise known as the bulk of the McHenry estate.

At the head of the valley, two small creeks tumbling down from alpine lakes join to form Aspen Creek, which undulates through a meadow a mile long and three quarters of a mile wide. At the foot of the meadow, the creek enters a forest of pines, aspens and cottonwoods and begins its descent to the East Buchanan River, several miles downstream. The ranch takes its name from the two creeks that become one, and cattle range throughout the meadow and occasionally beyond.

The ranch buildings sit at the foot of the valley and at the edge of the forest, with the creek running behind them. The main house, which faces southwest, is a quarter of a century old, about two thousand square feet, and made of sturdy blond pine wood, with a blue corrugated metal roof of the style popular in the mountains. A covered front porch, ten feet wide, runs along the length of the front, and a massive granite chimney pokes up from the left side of the house. Fifty yards away on one side is a large barn. On this evening, the space between it and the house was filled with the parked cars and trucks of those who had come for the barbecue. On the other side of the main ranch house, backing on to the creek, a half-dozen small cabins serve as residences for the cowhands or as guest cottages, such as the one Gordon occupied.

At a forty-five degree angle from the house and cabins, and across about 75 yards of open space, is another part of the forest. Here, beneath the shade of dozens of tall pines, is the spot the locals call McHenry Grove. About 15 weather-beaten tables, each capable of seating eight to ten people, are scattered in groupings of one, two, or three, roughly surrounding the barbecue pit, a circle of concrete five feet in diameter, with a retractable grill. Frank McHenry had built the pit and put in the tables 20 years ago to provide the setting for a fund-raising barbecue to build a youth center in Harperville, and that proved to be such a popular event that it continued to be held the last Saturday in June even after the center was built seven years ago. Other local groups were allowed to use the space to raise money for a good cause, or just to have a good time. As often as not Frank McHenry personally oversaw the activities, and could be found at the pit from sunup to well after sunset.

The McHenrys themselves typically held two large parties each summer. One was on the Fourth of July and the other was the Roundup Barbecue, the second Saturday of September to celebrate the successful fattening of the cattle at their summer pastures. A few hundred close friends, as well as ranch employees, were invited to each. Invariably the party would start early in the afternoon, and well after midnight there would still be a group of men playing poker by the dying coals of the fireplace. Most of the time, in years gone by, Frank McHenry or Mike Baca would be sitting in front of the biggest pile of chips.

The rains earlier in the week had left the ground just moistened enough not to be dusty. Friday had been a warm day, and Saturday afternoon at three o'clock it was 90 degrees but, owing to the dryness of the air, not too oppressive. The heat accentuated the smell of the dust and pine needles, which mingled with the odor of barbecue smoke. A half dozen children were taking refuge from the heat in a deep hole in the creek, and nearly 150 people were in the shade of the grove, downing beer and soft drinks. In spite of the unparalleled setting and the festive atmosphere, it seemed to Gordon that there was a certain edginess to the event, which he put down to local knowledge of the trial over the will. As he thought back on that day later, it flowed across his mind as a series of seemingly unconnected vignettes, the meaning and connection of which would not become clear until much later.

• • •

An hour before the barbecue began, Gordon's friend Sam Akers arrived from San Francisco. Sam could not have been more Gordon's opposite. Where Gordon was tall and athletic with rugged good looks, Sam was of medium height, owlish behind a set of round eyeglasses, and had spent a lifetime being one of the last players chosen for a team. Gordon was intense and analytical and had amassed a fortune through his shrewd investments. Sam was relaxed and cheerful and had worked twelve years for the same company, gradually reaching a reasonably well-paying middle management position. Gordon was a solitary man who had reached his mid thirties without encountering a serious challenge to his bachelorhood. Sam had married shortly out of college and had two children who were almost teenagers. As often happens with such temperamental opposites, they had become close friends and over the years developed an intimacy of understanding with each other.

As Sam unpacked in the cabin, Gordon told him about the barbecue and received a mild protest in return.

"Really," said Sam. "I've been looking forward to fishing all week and there are several hours of daylight left. Do we have to?"

"It'll be fun," Gordon said. "You don't get to do this sort of thing in the city. Besides," he said, dropping his voice almost imperceptibly, "I promised Ellen McHenry this morning that I'd be there."

"So you gave your word to a lady. She must be something special if she's worth giving up an afternoon of fishing."

"When did I say that?" snapped Gordon.

"You didn't, but it was pretty obvious. You have to remember that I've been listening to you talk about women for fifteen years now. I recognize new territory when I hear it."

"I admit I'm interested, but that's all. Nothing could happen in a place like this anyway. A waitress serves you two meals in a cafe and she can write your biography. This is a nice place to visit, but for regular living I prefer the anonymity of a city."

"I'll be interested to meet her," said Sam. "But tell me about the fishing."

"There hasn't been much to speak of. It rained pretty hard in the middle of the week, and the East Buchanan is still running murky, though I think it'll be all right by Monday. The smaller streams are running pretty clear. I went up to Mosquito Creek this morning and caught half a dozen fish in the six to ten inch range."

"Have you tried here?"

"No, I haven't, but Ellen said we're welcome to fish anywhere on the ranch. You want to give it a try tomorrow morning?"

"Twist my arm."

"And since it's uncharted water for both of us and we're on equal footing, how about a wager: Most fish caught by noon. Loser buys dinner at the Sportsman."

"Do you always have to compete?" asked Sam. "Why can't you just enjoy going fishing?"

"Come on. If it's a tie, it's still on me.

"Oh, all right. But you know you'll win. You always do."

"Breakfast's on me tomorrow."

"You're that sure of yourself?"

"Let's just say I'm feeling lucky. I have a feeling that tomorrow is going to be a great day to be alive."

• • •

That afternoon, Gordon discovered a new side of Ellen. It turned out that she had the knack of getting a man to relax and talk about himself, and her questions came across as expressions of genuine interest, rather than an attempt to make small talk.

"So how did you become a stockbroker?" she asked.

It occurred to Gordon that she had an unfair advantage in this regard, since he couldn't very well ask her how she came to be running a cattle ranch. They were standing in the picnic area amid other groups of people. He was sipping a beer, and she was drinking Dr. Pepper. She was wearing jeans, cowboy boots and a pink pocket T-shirt, and Gordon couldn't help feeling that her casual attire and command of the situation made her seem assured and attractive.

"Well," he said, "I'd like to say I planned for it all my life, but I'm afraid it's a little messier than that. The fact of the matter is that when I graduated from Cal twelve years ago, I had a degree in American history and the certain knowledge that I couldn't make a living playing basketball. The brokerage was just something I fell into."

"Fell into?"

"Maybe drawn into is more like it. In the Bay Area there are a fair number of businesses run by Cal grads. Some of them are willing to hire and train athletes who played for the old school. The president of the San Francisco office of Howell Burns & Bledsoe played basketball for Cal in the late 40s and still came to most of the games. Spring quarter of my senior year, once the basketball season was over, he called me in for an interview."

"That must have been nice."

"I don't think I fully appreciated it at the time. Anyway, he offered me a job when I graduated, and since I had to do something, I took it. I knew I could put in the hours and give it an effort, so it was a pleasant surprise to find out once I started that I actually enjoyed it and had some inclination for it."

Ellen McHenry shook her head. "The stock market is something I've never been able to understand, except for one thing. It's kind of like the cattle business, because the value of your assets fluctuates wildly from day to day due to of factors out of your control."

"That's true to a certain degree, but you have to remember the larger picture. If you do it intelligently and systematically, investing in the stock market amounts to betting on the economic growth of this country. And I don't know anybody who ever got rich by betting against America.

"I never thought of it that way. Tell me, do you have some sort of formula you follow?"

"For what?"

"I mean for deciding which stocks to pick and when to buy and when to sell."

"You want to know what I tell my clients? There are four basic rules to coming out ahead in the stock market. The first is to invest for the long term. You'll always lose money at some point, but time is your friend. Second, you protect yourself by diversifying. A good mix of stocks means the winners more than cover the losers. And third, stick with well-known, high quality stocks: blue chips, New York Stock Exchange."

"You said there were four rules."

"Rule number four," Gordon said with a hint of a smile, "is that you never, ever give your money to anybody over the phone."

"I'm curious now. Do you buy stocks for yourself, or after doing it all day for other people, do you want nothing to do with it?"

"I dabble a bit myself," he said softly. This was, in fact, an understatement. Gordon had joined the brokerage in the summer of 1981, and a year later decided that he was ready to try putting some of his own money into the market. In early August of 1982 he invested $10,000 in several stocks he thought were underpriced. The bull market of the eighties began a week later, and he continued to build his investments on a steady basis. His stock portfolio at the time he left for the fishing trip was worth five million dollars.

"Does anyone — I mean, just someone buying stocks for himself — ever get rich playing the market?" she asked.

"It can happen," he replied.

• • •

At the barbecue pit, Gordon, Sam and Baca were talking with Kitty Stevens. She had just finished turning a half-dozen large tri-tip steaks on the barbecue, after which she set the long barbecue fork carefully on the rim of the pit and lit a cigarette.

"Just enough time to sneak a smoke before these have to be turned again," she said. "Hope you don't mind."

Sam, who was trying, with little success, to find a spot not directly downwind of the barbecue smoke, said it was no problem. "Do you always do the cooking at these?" he asked.

"I have the last few years," she replied. "At least, I helped Frank. It just doesn't seem the same this year."

"Did you make plenty of chili?" asked Baca.

"Eight Dutch ovens. Think it'll last?"

"It never has." He turned to Gordon. "Kitty's chili is one of Summit County's treasures. I've always thought she could make a fortune distributing it nationally."

She smiled. "Thanks, but it wouldn't travel. My chili takes too much watching over to be mass-produced."

"I'm looking forward to trying it," Gordon said.

There was a long pause while she took a couple of drags on her cigarette. Baca watched her, with a gentle eye, then spoke softly.

"Going deer hunting this year, Kitty?"

She took another puff on the cigarette, then dropped it on the dirt and ground it out with her boot. "I don't know," she said. "I really don't know. What do you think, Mike?"

"I think you should. Get back on the horse that threw you and all that."

She turned to Gordon. "I'm sorry if we're being rude, it's just that I'm pretty close to this family. Frank and I used to go deer hunting together every fall. We'd start out from Costello Meadows, which is about eight thousand feet up. The family leases Forest Service land for pasture there and they have a little cabin where they or their hands spend the night sometimes. We'd leave that cabin before dawn and see who got the first deer, but it had to be a buck with at least four points."

"Kitty usually won," said Baca.

"Are you a good shot?" asked Gordon.

"Pretty good," she said. "But I think the difference was, I don't know how to say this, but I sort of think like a deer."

"How do you think like a deer?"

"I don't know, but I just had a sense that there might be something in the next ravine or whatever. Frank called it intuition."

"You don't like that word?"

"I guess it's as good as any. Do you boys hunt?"

Gordon shook his head. and Sam spoke up. "I don't like guns," he said. "I guess it's a city thing. And I think deer are kind of too pretty to shoot."

Kitty laughed. "Around here, deer kind of lose their novelty. If they weren't hunted, there'd be too many of them and they'd run out of food. And speaking of food, there are a lot of people around here who'd be hard pressed to get through the winter without the venison in their freezer."

"I never thought of that," said Sam.

"You have to live it to know it. That's why so many people here hate politicians. They're almost all from the city and they don't get it."

There was another pause. "Tell me," said Gordon, "Do you think there's much chance of a fisherman being mistaken for a deer and shot by a hunter?"

"I wouldn't think so," said Kitty. "Most hunters look out for that sort of thing." She picked up the fork and began to turn the meat again. Baca leaned over and whispered in Gordon's ear.

"Only if you're on the West Buchanan," he said.

• • •

The food, served from a makeshift buffet table at the edge of the grove, was simple and outstanding: slices of steak, Kitty's chili with beans, potato salad, tossed green salad, and biscuits. Gordon sat at the end of one table across from Ellen and Kitty, with Sam at his side. From time to time Gordon wondered about the relationship between these two women who had shared the love and affection of the same man, one as daughter, one as lover. He doubted if that was something they talked about much, or at all, yet there seemed to be an unspoken empathy between the two.

Ellen had steered the subject of the conversation to fishing, and was explaining about the creeks that ran through the ranch.

"Once you get upstream from the big meadow," she said, "the two feeder creeks are pretty small. You can have fun fishing for brook trout, but ten inches is a big fish and five or six is more like it most of the time."

"Has anybody ever caught a big fish up there?" Gordon asked.

"You know," she said, "now that you mention it, when I was a little girl, maybe seven or eight years old, I saw Dan catch a 16-inch trout about a half mile up one of them."

"So it can happen?"

"Must be. I remember that was early in the summer after a winter with a lot of snow. All the creeks were running higher than usual that year. I think Dan's fish just decided to head upstream and see what was there. He ended up being dinner, which shows you the danger of curiosity."

"That would have been more than 20 years ago," said Kitty. "There aren't as many fish as there used to be. Or water, it seems."

"But it's better once Aspen Creek starts?" Sam asked.

"Oh, sure." said Ellen. "The creek's bigger and the meadow gives the fish lots of grasshoppers and insects. I think there are a couple of Brown Trout two feet long in this meadow. They hang out under the banks or in the deep holes and only come out to feed at dusk. Most of what they eat is other fish, too. You may not see them, but they're there."

"How about below the meadow?" Gordon asked.

"It's more pocket water and not as buggy as the meadow," she said, "but there are some good fish in there." She looked him in the eye. "Have you tried the waters on the ranch yet?"

"No, I haven't, but maybe we should do that tomorrow. What do you say, Sam?"

"I'm easy."

"Let's go for it. Besides, it'll give you a new creek to fall into."

"Oh stop it."

"What's this?" asked Ellen.

"My friend is the world's unluckiest wader," Gordon said. "If there's a log in the creek he'll trip over it. If there's a slippery stone on the bottom, he'll step on it and fall in ass over teakettle. I've never seen anything like it."

"You're exaggerating," Sam said without conviction. "Besides, you don't know what it's like fishing with Gordon. I've known this man for fifteen years, and I can tell you that between luck and preparation, he almost never takes a false step. Fishing with somebody like that will drive you nuts. Living with him would, too. That's probably why he isn't married."

The ensuing silence brought Sam up short. Gordon was slowly rotating his bottle of beer on the wooden table. Kitty was scrutinizing a piece of meat on her fork with considerable intensity. Ellen was looking at Sam with her steady, penetrating gaze and a hint of a smile at the corners of her mouth.

"Yes," she said, after a few seconds. "Well, most of the fishing on this creek would be done from shore anyway, so you'll probably stay dry. With the mornings getting cooler, the fish will probably stay down until 8:30 or 9. I'll be heading into town around 9:30 — in fact almost everybody'll be gone tomorrow morning. But if no one's here, just fish wherever you like."

"Suits us," Gordon said. "We can sleep until a civil hour, have breakfast at Kitty's and start fishing when the fish get hungry."

"Oh! I just remembered something. My brother's going to be here tomorrow morning."

"Ellen! How could you?" This from Kitty in an exasperated voice.

"There's not much I can do to stop him. He came up to me before court on Thursday and said he'd like to go fishing at the ranch Sunday morning."

"You could have said no."

"Dad's last will granted Dan the use and enjoyment of the property. I'd be going against his wishes."

"Considering what your brother's been doing to you, he had a lot of nerve to ask," said Kitty.

"Are you sure he's going fishing?" Gordon asked.

"What do you mean?"

Her directness disarmed him, and he realized he had been drawn into the conversation more deeply than he had a right to be. He stumbled to find a way out.

"I'm not sure what I mean. Just with the lawsuit and all ..."

"Ah! You're thinking he might be after something. I hadn't thought of that, but it really doesn't bother me. I have nothing to hide, no matter what his expensive attorney tries to insinuate."

"Forget I said it."

"That's all right. And remember, there's more than enough water to fish. You don't have to be where Dan is."

• • •

"There are those who say there's still gold in some of those old mines, but I don't think so," said Mike Baca. It was dusk and the change of seasons was in the air. With the crowd at the barbecue beginning to thin out, he and Gordon were sitting alone at the end of a picnic table drinking black coffee from styrofoam cups.

"Where are the mines?" Gordon asked. "I've been up here quite a few times, and I don't remember seeing any."

"They're generally not on the beaten track, and they sort of honeycomb some of the canyons here. For instance, if you take the left fork of Aspen Creek and go upstream about a mile from this meadow, you'll find one on the left side of the canyon, but even then you have to know what you're looking for to see the entrance."

"Does anybody ever get lost in one?"

"Twice in the last 15 years. Those are the rescues I really hate. Some of these mines weren't propped up too well a hundred years ago, and they haven't gotten better with age."

"So where are the other mines?"

"As I said, all over the place. You know Costello Meadows?"

"I was up there once a few years ago, looking for a place to fish."

"The meadow is one of the McHenry family's summer pastures. And about a mile and a half down the road from it is a flat area, about four acres altogether. Would you believe that in 1888, there was a city of two thousand people there. That was the height of the gold boom here. And in 1890, when they took the census, it was gone. Just like that."

"Funny, you don't see any sign of it."

"It was mostly tents. The man who owned the general store was halfway through putting up a permanent building when people stopped finding gold. That was in early July, and by the time winter rolled around he was about the only one left."

"What a story."

"I could tell you more, but they'll have to wait." Baca drained his coffee cup and stood up. "The poker game's getting going inside. With Frank McHenry gone, I'm afraid it won't last as long as it used to, but I'll still be expected to play a few hands. Can you excuse me for at least an hour."

"That's fine. I can keep myself busy for an hour."

A flicker of a smile crossed Baca's face. "I'm sure you can," he said.

• • •

It was dark. The crickets provided constant background noise, and from time to time a gust of wind rattled through the pines and aspens, sending leaves and needles to the ground. A half moon hung overhead, lighting up the sky, but not entirely obscuring the stars that can be seen with such clarity through the thin mountain air. It was a night to quicken the pulse, but Ellen McHenry was staving off melancholy as she addressed the topic she had, up to this point in the evening, been able to avoid.

"It's scary," she said. "And so wrong. So fundamentally wrong. You were there on Thursday. You heard it. I listened to that lawyer asking all those questions, and even though the facts were more or less right, it came out sounding wrong. I was trying to help my father, and they made it look like I was pushing him into something he didn't want to do, didn't they?"

"I don't know," said Gordon. "It's hard to say. I only heard a bit of testimony, and I don't know what came before it and how it fits in."

"You're trying to be kind, but you know it looked bad. I'm afraid I don't have much hope."

Gordon didn't answer. They were on the covered porch of the main house, sitting on chairs that had been turned at a 45-degree angle partially facing each other. He became aware of his closeness to her and pushed himself all the way back in his chair.

"I never imagined something like this happening to me," she continued after a moment. You think the courts are there to deliver justice, but they seem to provide a place where whoever has the best lawyer can get what he wants. You said your father's a judge — how does he feel about it?"

"My father very much believes in what he does, but he understands that the legal system is imperfect. He's said many times that the best attorneys are the ones who keep their clients from going in front of him."

"I wish my brother had a lawyer like that." She shook her head. "I don't think Dan appreciates what he's put our family through. It was hard enough when we found out he was gay. I don't understand that, but I accept that it's what he is and not some choice he made. But getting involved with that posse crowd and Rex Radio was what really did it. Do you know anything about them?"

"A little," said Gordon, and he briefly recounted his story of the encounter the morning before and the conversation in the bar the previous evening. "Radio is a strange one," he concluded. "He's created his own legend, which a lot of us do, but he's started to believe in it himself, and that can be dangerous. On top of which he has the personality of a rattlesnake dipped in honey."

"Those men are evil," she said. "I'm more or less lapsed from the church, but I do believe in the existence of evil, and I think the first place to look for it is in the hearts and minds of people who know for a fact that they're right and everybody else is wrong. My father would agree with that, too. He was a conservative Republican, but he accepted the authority that comes from the democratic process, even when he disagreed with it. He had no use for the people Dan's fallen in with."

"What do you think they're up to?"

"There's not a doubt in my mind. They want this ranch for their posse games and God knows what else. It took us a while to realize that. Dad had talked about changing his will before, but he was healthy and he thought Dan would come to his senses, so he never did anything about it."

"Then all those conversations in the hospital really weren't the first time the matter came up?"

"Of course not. Dad was in shock then. If he'd been any less tough, he wouldn't even have gotten to the hospital alive. But he knew what he had to do, and what he really wanted to do. And for giving him encouragement and doing the things he was too weak to do for himself, I've been dragged through the mud.

"Haven't you been able to testify? Your story should carry some weight."

She laughed derisively. "They'll be calling me on Monday. So I'll take the stand and tell the truth, and my brother's attorney will find a way to make that look like something awful. I'd give anything not to have to face that attorney on the witness stand. I'd kill to have this whole thing go away. This place means everything to me, and I can't stand to think of losing it."

From the open front door a dozen feet away, there was the sound of a match being lit. Ellen turned, and Gordon, who was already looking in that direction, saw Mike Baca lighting a cigarette.

"Beautiful evening, isn't it?" said the sheriff.

Gordon and Ellen agreed that it was.

"Ellen," said Baca, "you've outdone yourself. It was a great barbecue, and I've had a fine time. But troublemakers never sleep, and I have to be up early, so I think I'll be on my way. Thank you for everything."

"Thanks for being here, Mike," Ellen said. "You made it feel like old times again for a few hours."

"Oh, and Gordon: I don't know if your friend Sam always plays poker like this ..."

"He does."

"You might want to get him away from the table before he loses any more than he has. Good night, kids." Gordon watched Baca walk away toward the barn, where his car was parked. The sheriff had put on some weight over the years, but he still walked with a graceful economy that bespoke authority. Gordon thought, looking after him, that the man could be elected sheriff anywhere on the basis of that walk alone.

"I don't want to go now," Gordon said, standing up, "but it sounds as if Sam needs my calming presence."

"Not at all," said Ellen, getting up herself. "I have to make the rounds, too." She paused and looked up into his eyes.

"There's something I have to tell you," she said. "I was very rude to you on the way out of court the day before yesterday, and I apologize for that. But I really appreciated the way you handled it. Some men would have snapped back at me and some would have just taken the abuse. You stood up for yourself, but you did it like a gentleman. Thanks.

"Gentleman?" said Gordon. "That's another one of those words, like 'honor,' that you don't hear too much these days.

She smiled. "I was talking too much, but it was nice to have someone here to listen. I'll see you and your friend tomorrow morning, and may you have a day of fishing you'll never forget."

• • •

"Living with him would drive you nuts," said Gordon sarcastically. "That's probably why he isn't married. Thanks a lot, Sam. If this is what your friends do to you ..."

Sam had taken a bottle of brandy out of his suitcase and was pouring two fingers into a tumbler. He handed it to Gordon.

"Here. This'll make you feel better." He poured one for himself. "Besides, she might as well know the truth up front." He raised his glass. "To honest and open relationships." They each took a swallow. "How much did I lose in the poker game?"

"Seventy five dollars," said Gordon, "and the way you were playing you got off easy. Judy's going to kill you."

"No she won't," said Sam. "Seventy five dollars isn't capital punishment — it's life in purgatory. What was I doing wrong, anyway?"

Gordon put his hand over his eyes and rubbed his forehead. "Listen up, Sam. The hand I stood behind you, you had the five of diamonds, the six of hearts, the seven of spades, the nine of diamonds and the king of spades. So what did you do?"

"What else could I do? I tossed the king and drew a card."

"That's right. You drew on an inside straight. Since you only had a dollar in the pot, it might have been worth a flyer. But what card did you draw?"

"Three of clubs."

"Which left you holding a hand with no pair, no flush, no straight, and your high card is a nine. Does that seem like a winner to you?"

"Of course not."

"So when the next round of betting started, why did you see the first five and raise it five?"

"Don't be obtuse, Gordon. Haven't you ever heard of a bluff? I took out three of the other four players right there."

"Precisely. And why do you think the fourth one was still in the game?"

"He wanted to play."

"Sam! The fourth man was in the game because he had something better than a nine-high in his hand. You were toast."

"He might not have called my bluff."

"If you're holding four kings, you're not going to be bluffed. Look, Sam, you have to learn to cut your losses. When you drew the three, you should have bailed out and kissed off the dollar you already had in. Cutting your losses intelligently is the key to success. Do you know the first thing I do when I buy a stock?"

"What?"

"I put an automatic sell order on it. If it falls fifteen percent below what I paid for it, it's gone. That way I still have eighty five percent of the money to invest again."

Sam eyed his friend warily. "Don't you ever do something just on impulse, Gordon?"

"Not if I can help it."

They sipped their brandy in intimate silence for a few minutes, then Gordon got up and walked the few steps to the door and opened it. He stepped outside, looked up at the moon through the branches of the pine trees, and took a deep breath of the bracing mountain air. Sam came out and joined him. The temperature had dropped into the high forties and the only noise that could be heard was the sound of the creek. A dim light burned in one room of the main ranch house.

"I've only been here a couple of days," Gordon said at last, "but I really like this place. It has the magic."

Sam wisely said nothing.

Sunday September 12

The day dawned clear and cold, and when Gordon and Sam arose shortly before seven o'clock there was a thin layer of frost on their car windows, the picnic tables and the meadow beyond the ranch house. They drove to Mom's cafe and found it nearly empty, but warm and inviting nonetheless. After Kitty's dissection of him two days earlier, Gordon was planning on ordering something completely different, but when he learned she wasn't in, he backed off and called for bacon, scrambled eggs and hash browns. He and Sam were in a hearty mood when they returned to Twin Creek Ranch at eight thirty. There was still frost on the grass of the meadow, but the sun had just come over the mountain and would soon melt it away. As they arrived, Gordon noticed that there was a lone man in a red chamois shirt fishing the creek about three quarters of the way up the meadow.

Ellen McHenry greeted them with an offer of coffee, which they declined. She was dressed as the day before, only this time the color of her T-shirt was teal and only the tip of the crew neck showed above the top of the gray wool sweater she wore over it. She had a large coffee mug, obviously made at a pottery studio, in her hand, and she used it to gesture toward a red pickup with gray trim parked a short distance from the house.

"Dan got here first," she said. "You probably saw him fishing up the meadow a ways." She paused. "You're welcome to do the same if you like, but if you're not feeling sociable, downstream might be the way to go."

Gordon nodded.

"I'll be leaving for town in half an hour, but before I go, here's a suggestion," she said. "About a quarter mile downstream from the last cottage, you'll come to a slight bend in the creek where an undercut bank's been carved out right under the roots of an old pine tree. There's a big Brown Trout — maybe eighteen inches long — that lives there. He's nobody's fool, but about once a year one of the boys hooks him. Give him a try if you like."

"How deep's the water?" Gordon asked.

"Hard to say. There's a nice little pocket there. At this time of year I'd guess maybe three feet but I could be off by a foot in either direction. Why?"

"I like to be prepared," Gordon said.

After taking their leave, Gordon and Sam fished their way downstream, each man stopping at a likely spot and working it for several casts, while the other leap-frogged ahead to the next likely spot. At the third spot he tried, Gordon worked his way around to the foot of a pool about 20 feet long, crouched low in the water and zinged a perfect cast to the base of a rock, where the water tumbled down from a foot above. It was instantly smacked by a ten-inch rainbow trout, who put up a vigorous fight before being brought to hand and released. It was a native, beautifully colored, and Gordon held it in the water for a moment, admiring its beauty before releasing it.

Five minutes later, in a piece of slightly faster water downstream, Sam cast a fly perfectly under an overhanging tree branch and was rewarded with a trout of similar size and coloring. In an effort to repeat his good fortune, he made two casts in the same direction and lost a fly in the tree each time. A short time afterward, Gordon made a deft cast to the top of a chute of water coming through a pool and watched a fish take the fly as it swirled down the current. When he got that fish in, Gordon noted from the dark speckles on its top that it was a brook trout. It was only a nine-inch fish, but it was a rarity in the area and he was pleased at having caught and released it.

In this fashion they reached the cut under the pine tree in a little under an hour. Gordon surveyed the water from above, then moved to the side of it, keeping well back and out of sight of any fish. Finally, he met Sam again at the top of the run.

"Well," said Sam. "That sure looks like a place there'd be a nice fish. Who goes first?"

Gordon took a quarter out of his pants pocket and flipped it end over end in the air. "Call it," he said.

"Tails."

The coin landed on its side on a small rock by the creek, bounced into the air, and fell into six inches of water before coming to rest on the bottom. The two men peered through the creek at it.

"Heads," said Sam. "Fair enough. I think I'll take a break from fishing and watch you try your luck."

"Skill, you mean. If you're not fishing, could you hold my rod while I change flies."

"What's wrong with what you have on?"

"Sam, this is a number 12 Royal Wulff."

"It's caught two fish already."

"And those two fish would be a snack for what I'm going after now. Here." He led Sam to a shallow, heavily pebbled section of the creek above the spot he was preparing to fish. "See this?" He pointed with his rod to a black spot on a light-colored rock, then scraped it off with his rod tip. "Stonefly nymph, I'm guessing about number 6. They're everywhere in this creek. Mr. Brown Trout, if he's in there, is probably sitting near the bottom sucking these in by the dozen as the current carries them through his water." He took a fly box from his vest and removed a black fly half an inch long, and about the same shape and color as the nymphs on the rock. "This is the ticket."

Gordon snipped off the fly on his line, then cut two feet of 5X tippet from the end of his leader and retied it back where it was.

"Why are you doing that?" Sam asked.

"To get a knot up here. You'll see." Gordon then reached into his vest and took out some lighter 6X tippet material and attached that to the reattached 5X with a sound knot. He trimmed the 6X tippet six inches below the bottom knot. "Now we're getting there," he said. Reaching into his vest again he pulled out a bright-orange bobber about three-eighths of an inch in diameter and a toothpick. A narrow passage ran through the axis of the bobber, and Gordon threaded the end of the leader through it. When he had gotten it over the knot at the top of the 5X leader, he pushed the toothpick into the passage with the leader. Once the tip of the toothpick showed through the bottom end, he snapped off the top of it about a quarter-inch from the bobber. He tied on the black nymph and finally removed a package of BB-sized weights from his vest and clamped one on the leader just above the bottom knot and inches from the fly.

Sam watched with fascination. "You're certainly cleaning out the hardware store," he said. "Would you care to tell me what it's all about."

"Simple," said Gordon. "I'm trying to bring that fly down to Mr. Fish along that current near the bottom. The weight gets the fly down fast, and the cork bobber serves both as an indicator — to tell you when something's touching the fly — and fixes the depth based on where it's located on the line. Nothing to it."

"Let's see it work."

Gordon moved himself into position slowly and carefully. The pine tree was on the eastern shore of the creek so the sun was in front of him and his shadow wouldn't hit the water. Even so, he proceeded quietly and kept a low profile until he had reached a spot on the bank directly across from where he believed the fish to be. There was a gravelly beach about five feet wide on his side, which earlier in the season had probably been under a couple of inches of water. He squatted at the back of it to stay as low and far away as possible and was relieved to notice that there was no brush directly behind him, so he could make a reasonably unimpeded cast.

Aspen Creek, at this point, was twenty feet wide. After cascading through some boulders, the water leveled out into a riffle about twenty feet above the pine tree, with its main current running about a foot from the opposite bank. The system he had rigged up was cumbersome, but after a couple of tries, he found that by casting long and to the top of the riffle, he could drag his indicator and fly into the main current and let them drift cleanly over the hole under the pine tree. He did this six times without attracting the interest of a fish.

"I hate to be the one to say this," said Sam, "but it looks like you just went to a lot of trouble for nothing."

"That was just a dress rehearsal. I had the fly at two and a half feet, and it's probably too high for the fish to see. I'm going to move that indicator up six inches and see what happens."

On his second cast, Gordon hit the spot he wanted at the top of the riffle and got the indicator and fly drifting cleanly down the current. As the orange bobber glided beneath the edge of the undercut bank, it suddenly went under water. Gordon raised his rod tip, and what he hooked was so solid that for an instant he thought the fly had become embedded in the bottom. Then he felt a violent twitch and realized he had a fish on.

It streaked upstream, tearing a few feet of line from Gordon's reel, but the cascade above blocked its passage, and Gordon helped a bit by pulling to his right to turn the fish's head away from the one gap in the rocks through which it might conceivably have gone. As he did so, the trout came close to the surface, and he could see that it was as good a fish as Ellen McHenry had said. It went back downstream to its hiding place and thrashed backward and forward, attempting to shed the hook from its lip. But Gordon kept steady pressure on the line, and when the fish let up for a second, Gordon deftly used his rod to turn its head in the opposite direction to wear it down. The trout made a dash downstream, but encountered a stretch of shallow water that left it badly exposed, so Gordon was able to turn it back towards him again. After more head-shaking and zig-zagging in its little corner of the stream, the fish was showing signs of fatigue, and Gordon began slowly pulling it toward him. After a couple of shakes and runs, it rolled over on its side as he pulled it up to the bank. He handed his rod to Sam, who had come over for a better look, and knelt over the fish, which was now lying in three inches of water. It was a beautifully colored German Brown, golden in hue and dappled with red and black spots. The hook of Gordon's fly was neatly piercing its right upper lip.

"Wow!" said Sam. "Well done."

"I don't suppose you brought your camera?"

"No, I didn't."

"Then I guess we'll just have memories." Gordon knelt over the large trout and reached for the fly. The fish flapped a couple of times, and he said, "Hold steady, here. You'll be home again in no time."

A gunshot rang out in the distance, like a thunderclap reverberating through the small mountain valley. Gordon and Sam both froze, then Gordon smiled. "Deer hunters, probably." He reached down again and with a quick flick of his wrist removed the barbless hook from the fish's lip. With his left hand, he moved the fish farther out into the current and held it gently upright, facing upstream. The trout's gills opened and closed quickly as it pumped oxygen into its system, getting its breath back. After about two minutes it streaked out of Gordon's hand, made a sharp left turn, and headed back under the overhanging pine tree.

"That was a beautiful fish," said Sam.

"Best I've caught this trip." Gordon bent down to pick up his rod, and as he did so he was conscious of a vehicle driving above them on the dirt road leading out of the ranch. The creek was about 40 feet below the road at this point, and the angle was such that they couldn't see the road directly. He assumed it must have been Ellen McHenry heading into town, though as he looked at his watch he realized it was ten o'clock — an hour after she said she'd be going. He looked up again and could see only a puff of dust left by the passing vehicle. Then he shrugged and turned his attention back to fishing.

After the capture and release of the Brown Trout, the rest of the morning was anticlimactic. Gordon and Sam each landed some small to medium fish; the morning ended with Gordon two fish ahead and winning the dinner bet. When they returned to the main ranch house at a quarter past noon, both men felt they had enjoyed a half-day that had restored their spirits and left them with the pleasurable feeling of physical lassitude and contentment that good exercise and fresh air can bring.

They stopped to thank their hostess but found she hadn't yet returned. In fact, there seemed to be no one present, either in the house itself or the surrounding cabins. Dan McHenry's pickup was still parked near the house, but he wasn't visible in the meadow. Noticing this, Gordon nudged Sam.

"Are you in any hurry for lunch?"

"I can wait a bit. Why?"

"It looks like Dan McHenry's gone upstream and left the meadow to us. Let's check it out."

The sun had long since burned the frost off the grass, but even though it was mid-day, a cool breeze out of the north kept it from being hot. The meadow was full of grasshoppers that jumped to all sides as the two men walked through it, leading Sam to remark that it might not be a bad idea to fish an imitation hopper close to a grassy bank. Gordon agreed. They went halfway up the meadow, prospecting for likely fish lies. Then, as they came to a previously obscured bend, Gordon saw a flash of red.

He stopped and tensed as he focused on it and realized what he was seeing. Where the creek made a horseshoe bend, it had carved out a deep pool, at the foot of which a large shrub, growing from the side of the bank, overhung the water and actually dipped several branches into it. The current had carried the body of a man — the body of Dan McHenry, to be precise — into the bush where it had become grotesquely entangled. The left shoulder, covered by the red chamois shirt, was propped out of the water, while his head, eyes fixed with a vacant stare, lay in the water being rocked slowly back and forth by the gentle, eddying current. At a cursory glance, it might have looked as if he had drowned, but through the thin latticework of branches that held McHenry in place, the back of his shirt could be seen clearly enough to show that there was a sizable hole below that left shoulder, almost directly behind the heart. It was the sort of hole that a high-caliber bullet might have made as it entered or left the body. Gordon pulled up short with a shiver of revulsion. Sam, who had been talking, also stopped, then looked where Gordon was pointing. When he saw the body, his eyes widened and his mouth opened, but nothing came out. Reflexively, he took a step backward, but since he was at the edge of the creek, his foot touched nothing but air and he fell backwards into two feet of cold water with a loud splash.

That had the effect of prying Gordon's eyes and mind off the body for a moment. Sam had landed in a riffle and been washed ten feet downstream before he was able to right himself. He was utterly soaked as Gordon moved toward him.

"Are you all right."

"A damn sight better than he is," Sam said, pointing in the direction of Dan McHenry. He climbed back on to the meadow, dripping wet. "This is horrible. What do we do now?"

"We get back and call the sheriff. Now. Double time. They began to jog across the meadow, as fast as their fishing gear would allow. As they moved, Gordon couldn't help thinking that, although it had happened in a nasty and bloody fashion, the dispute over the McHenry inheritance had been resolved once and for all. He tried to put the thought out of his mind, but it wouldn't budge.

They arrived breathlessly at the ranch house, just as Ellen pulled up in her pickup. She stepped out and greeted them cordially.

"Did you boys switch places with Dan?" she asked. "His truck's here, but I didn't see him in the meadow on the way in."

Gordon hesitated for a second, then decided to give her the news straight.

"We need to call the sheriff, Ellen. Your brother's dead."

Her right hand shot up to her mouth. "Oh, God, no!"

He took her by the left arm. "Let's go," he said softly.

She shook his hand away. "How did it happen?"

He tried to be soothing. "I think you should get inside and we should call the sheriff."

"Don't protect me, Gordon. He's my brother and I want to know what happened."

He hesitated a moment, then said, "It looks as if he was shot."

Ellen stiffened and a flash of steel came into her eyes. "Those bastards," she said. "Those fascist bastards."

• • •

The next few hours went by at a gallop. Sheriff Baca presided over the situation with calmness and professionalism, but so much was happening and so many people were coming and going — seeking orders or bearing information — that it would have made anyone's head spin. Baca had activated every deputy and reserve and called in the fire department and Highway Patrol. Dan McHenry was beyond help, but Baca was relentless in his efforts to ensure that his killer would not escape for want of manpower.

He commandeered a vacant cabin (next to Gordon and Sam's) for conducting interviews, and beginning at 2:30 spoke at length with, first, Ellen McHenry, then Sam Akers. For two hours, Gordon sat in the picnic area that had hosted the festive gathering less than 24 hours earlier. From it, he had a good view of the main house, Baca's cabin, and the meadow, now swarming with people who were combing the grass, earth and water for any scrap of evidence. Gordon drank several bottles of soft drinks and looked on with a sense of numbness and incomprehension. He felt he could really use a beer and could have taken one from his ice chest, but he was determined to wait until after his interview with the sheriff.

It was four-thirty when he was finally called. The interior of the cabin was ten feet by fifteen. It was sparsely furnished with two twin beds, two chairs, and a sink that drew its water from the creek via a pump handle. There were two windows along one of the long walls, and along the other a row of wooden pegs (for hanging clothing and saddle paraphernalia), with a one-foot shelf protruding above. The two beds had been pushed against the far wall and the two chairs turned to face them. In one chair sat Baca and in the other a young deputy named Joe, who, as the interview went along, took notes on a laptop computer.

Baca led Gordon through his story carefully, paying particular attention to the gunshot and the car driving by. He returned to those points after Gordon's had gone over the morning in detail.

"So you'd just caught this really nice trout, which was how big?"

"Nineteen inches."

"Nineteen inches. I thought you said eighteen inches the first time."

"He did, sir." Joe didn't look up from the computer as he said this.

"I didn't have time to measure him," Gordon snapped. "What difference does it make?"

"In the solution of this crime, probably none. But it's a very interesting side point to those of us who live here. Anyway, you were getting ready to unhook him when you heard the shot. Right?"

"That's right."

"How loud was it and what did you think it was?"

"It was loud enough, and there was a bit of an echo, I remember that. But it obviously wasn't really close by. I just assumed it was a deer hunter."

"Could you tell what direction it was coming from?"

"It seemed like generally towards the house and meadow."

"How sure are you?"

"Fairly sure, but I can't be certain. Sometimes it's hard to tell."

"Do you have any idea what time this happened?"

"I can pin that pretty close. I looked at my watch right after the car went by above us, and it was ten o'clock then. The shot must have been fired five minutes earlier, give or take a minute or two."

"Okay, about this car driving by, did you see any part of it at all?"

"I've been racking my brains, and I really can't think of anything. You have to remember I was concentrating on fishing. I just remember seeing the slightest bit of dust coming over the edge of the road."

"Think harder. Anything you can give us — even the slightest detail — could be absolutely critical."

"I've tried., Mike. I can't remember anything. If I do, you'll be the first to know."

Baca was holding a cheap ballpoint pen in his right hand. He tapped it on the arm of his chair a few times in impatience or irritation.

"All right," he said, "I'll back off on that for now. But I need the best answer you can give to the next question, too. Did you hear or see any other car go by while you were fishing?"

"Nothing."

"You didn't see or hear Ellen McHenry's truck go by before the shot?"

"No, but that doesn't mean anything."

"I'll be the judge of that."

"Look, when we first started fishing, just below the house, the creek was curving away from the road, and it was moving fast and making a fair amount of noise. It's not very likely either Sam or I would have heard or seen anything. It was only when we got down by where I caught the big fish that we were getting even with the road again. Anybody could have come or gone that first hour and a half we were out there."

"Maybe," said Baca. He tapped his arm rest with the pen again, then turned to the deputy. "We're done with this witness for now. Why don't you go over to the house and see if they can rustle up a pot of coffee for us? If the answer's yes, bring back three cups."

The deputy folded up his computer, put it in a case, and trudged off toward the main house. Neither man spoke until he had been gone for two minutes, then Gordon broke the silence.

"So what do you think?"

"None of your business what I think. You ought to know that. Still, I want a word with you off the record."

"You suspect Ellen, don't you?"

"I haven't reached a conclusion and evidence is far from in. What we have is a man who was killed in a wide open space in broad daylight, and the fact is that almost anyone in this county could have done it. There are five churches in town, and they all start their Sunday services at 10:30 or 11 in the morning. If the shot you heard was the one that killed Dan McHenry, the killer could have been in church singing hymns an hour later, with no one the wiser."

"Is that really what you think?"

"It's a possibility I have to consider." Baca looked at his watch, then out the window toward the house. "Look, I have no right to be talking to you about this, but I'm going to anyway because I don't want you getting in my way or causing trouble. And if anybody asks, this conversation never happened."

"What conversation?"

"Thank you. Now listen. To someone else, you could be a potential suspect, but right now I'm writing you off for three reasons. First, you have a witness who can give you an alibi; second, I know for a fact that you don't like guns or have any experience using them; and third because your motive is pretty marginal."

"Thanks for the vote of confidence."

"Save the sarcasm and listen, but don't breathe a word of this to anybody. From what we can tell right now, Dan McHenry was shot from a distance of 150 yards with a high-caliber rifle. The bullet didn't go through the body, which is nothing less than an absolute miracle, and the medical examiner said she's pretty sure it's from a 30.06."

"Where was the shot fired from?"

"Whoever did it got an angle above and behind him. And there's one way you could do that. Just past the cattle guard when you get to the ranch, there's a rough dirt road that goes off to the right and runs through the trees on the opposite edge of the meadow from the creek, going to a cattle pen at the top of the meadow. Based on where we found his fishing rod, it looks like somebody drove up there, took dead aim on him and fired one shot that hit him in the back and came out through the bottom of his heart. I'm guessing he died immediately or bled out in a couple of minutes. We'll know when the coroner checks his lungs for water."

"So really anybody could have gone up that road and fired the shot."

"Anybody who knew about it, which probably reduces the list of suspects to about half the county."

"How about the gun itself? Is there any chance of tracing it?"

"If we find a likely rifle, we can compare it against the bullet easily enough, but you have to realize that a 30.06 is one of the most commonly used deer rifles in the state of California. Probably half the people in the county own one."

"Wouldn't there be tire tracks or some evidence along that road?"

"We're looking, of course, but I'm not hopeful. It's a hard road with as much rock as dirt on the surface. And it's only in cheap novels that killers drop monogrammed handkerchiefs at the scene of the crime."

"So it could have been anyone?"

"It could have been anyone, but it had to be someone. And when we try to find that someone, we go back to the basics. That means looking for motive, means, and opportunity."

Gordon felt his stomach tighten.

"When you look at it that way," Baca said, "there's one person who comes quickly to mind."

"Ellen."

"I'm afraid so. It looked as if she was going to lose the ranch to her brother. That's motive. She has a house full of guns and knows how to use them. Last year, she won a gold medal in marksmanship at the County Fair. That's means. And she can't prove she wasn't here at around the time the crime occurred. That's opportunity."

"That's also pure speculation."

"It isn't enough evidence to make an arrest, but there are several other interesting points to be considered. First of all, there's the matter of the missing gun."

"What?"

"There's a gun missing from a locked gun case in the main house. Ellen McHenry has no idea how long it might have been gone and claims it's the one her brother used to use for deer hunting. It happens to be a 30.06."

Gordon exhaled loudly.

"Then there's the matter of an alibi. She says she left the house some time between 9:30 and 9:45 and went into town. According to her, she stopped at Kitty Stevens' house to talk, but — guess what? — nobody was home. By the time she got to the grocery store, where somebody could vouch for her presence, it was ten thirty. She could have left the ranch at ten and done that, and even had time for a small stop to dispose of something."

Gordon listened in sullen silence. After pausing briefly to let the last point sink in, Baca continued.

"On top of all that, there's something a bit strange about the situation that led up to the crime. Considering what she and her brother are going through, why did she let him come up here and fish in the first place? Everybody who heard about that thought it was strange. And then there's what she said to you last night."

"Said to me?"

"Don't tell me you've forgotten. Just as I was leaving, she said, 'I'd kill to have this whole thing go away. I love this place too much, and I can't stand to think of losing it. Especially to that bunch.' Pretty strong language."

"Oh, come on," said Gordon, his anger rising. "That was just talk and you know it."

"I don't know anything," said Baca. "I'm just a dumb sheriff, so I try to collect all the facts and information I can and hope it leads me somewhere. And right now it's pretty clear where this is leading."

"She didn't do it."

"Gordon, come on."

"She didn't do it. I just know."

"Listen. It's obvious to me and to anybody else who had eyes and used them last night that you two kids are attracted to each other. That's not surprising. You're both nice people, and from her point of view you'd be a better catch than the slim pickings around here. But you don't really know her, and you have no business getting involved in this investigation, emotionally or otherwise. So stay out of it, and as a friend I'm asking you to leave her alone, at least for now. Trust me. It's the best way to do it."

Gordon sat silently, noticing that the bunkhouse had gotten noticeably darker since he first came in. Finally, he said, "I'll take your advice on the investigation, at least. That's your business. But do you really think she has the character to commit a crime like this?"

Now it was Baca's turn to pause before answering. "I'd like to think not, I really would. And maybe some evidence will come up that will turn me in a different direction. You know, Ellen's a nice lady, but there's one thing I feel in my gut. This murder was committed by someone the world has been regarding as a decent person."

• • •

Gordon was in a sullen mood as he and Sam waited for their steaks to be served at the Sportsman. It was eight o'clock and he'd had nothing to eat since breakfast twelve hours earlier, but he was too tense to be really hungry. He was consumed with what Baca had said, and kept turning it over in his mind in the hopes that, viewed from a different angle, the facts would suggest something other than what they did.

The waitress brought their steaks (Gordon's cooked medium-well and Sam's medium-rare), and their pungent aroma finally caused Gordon's appetite to return. This was cattle country, and the chef at the Sportsman knew how to do beef justice, so the two men were soon enjoying their meal and temporarily setting aside the murder of Dan McHenry. When they were about three quarters done, the waitress brought them two more bottles of beer.

"We didn't order these," said Sam.

"I know," said the waitress. "They were sent by a gentleman in the bar."

Gordon turned to look at the door to the bar behind him. Hart Lee Bowen was standing by it, and acknowledged the attention by smiling and touching the brim of his hat."

"What's this all about?" asked Sam.

"I think we've been summoned for an audience with the great man."

"You mean ..."

"Rex Radio himself. Come on; let's finish up. I want to hear what he has to say."

They ate the rest of the meal quickly and took their half-finished bottles of beer into the bar. It was half empty, and Radio, Bowen, and George Horton were occupying the same corner table they'd been at two nights ago. As Gordon walked up to the table, he looked closely at Horton. In a way, he was closer to Dan McHenry than anyone else had been over the past few years, and his face betrayed a look of shock. Gordon wondered how he had taken the news.

"This is my friend Sam Akers," he said, "and we're both grateful for the beers. But the next round's on me. I insist."

Radio waved his hand. "Don't worry," he said. "Nobody's keeping count. I just wanted to say hello and thought this would be a good way to get the conversation going." He leaned forward conspiratorially. "I hear you caught a 22-inch trout in the creek below the McHenry house this morning."

"You must have gotten the news at some remove. Eighteen inches is more like it."

"A fine fish nevertheless. You're obviously a world-class angler."

"Did you really bring me in here to talk about fishing?"

"Partly. But if you're getting impatient ..."

"I am."

"All right, then. Let's move on to the next thing. Danny McHenry meant a lot to me. He was almost like a son." Horton glared at him. "I'd feel a lot better just hearing what happened from you directly."

"Sorry. Can't talk. Sheriff's orders."

"Of course. I should have expected it. Anyway, the word on the street is that they're about to make an arrest pretty soon."

"Who told you that?"

"Now don't get excited. It does seem that everything points at his sister. I sure would hate for that to be true. She seems like such a nice young lady." He paused. "Stubborn and opinionated, but nice. I sure hope nothing unpleasant happens to her."

"Like hay dropping from a barn door?" said Sam innocently.

Radio gave Sam a contemptuous stare, then continued, "Anything could happen, of course, but I have a feeling that Miss McHenry's troubles are more apt to be of the legal variety than in the occupational safety line."

"You're blowing smoke," Gordon said. "Almost anybody could have gone up there and fired that shot. "For that matter, where were you at ten o'clock this morning?"

Radio's body tensed and his eyes narrowed, but he kept himself under control. "Me? I was at our camp on the West Buchanan with about ten witnesses watching me the whole time. That's nine more than you have."

Gordon enjoyed having drawn a reaction, and he quickly thought of another arrow to fire. "Anyway," he said, "I guess that whatever else it did, the death of Dan McHenry ..."

"Murder," Radio said.

"The death of Dan McHenry at least ended the legal challenge to the will."

"Wrong."

"Wrong?" It was Gordon's turn to flinch.

"That may have been what certain people had in mind, but it's not over yet. The situation has been complicated, to be sure, but it's not over."

"I don't understand," Gordon said.

"The week before the trial started, Dan McHenry decided it was about time for him to make his own will, so he did. After a few modest bequests, the bulk and residue of the estate was left to — yours truly."

"You!" shouted Horton. "You?"

"Control yourself, George, or I'm going to have to send you out to buy some groceries. That's right. He left everything to me, and an hour ago," he took his cellular phone out of a jacket pocket and gestured toward Gordon and Sam with it, "I talked to my attorney. As Dan McHenry's heir and beneficiary, I have full legal authority to pursue any and all claims on his behalf, including the challenge to his father's will." He pounded the phone down on the table. "Which I have every intention of doing."

Monday September 13

Some time in the middle of the night, Gordon found himself awake and listening to the noises outside the cabin. The steady roar of the creek was foremost, but he thought he heard an engine running in the distance. He moved over to the window to look, but saw nothing unusual, and after a few minutes returned to bed and fell asleep.

At ten o'clock in the morning the attorneys in the McHenry lawsuit appeared before Judge Hawkins for three minutes. All parties agreed that in light of Dan McHenry's murder the trial should be recessed for a week. Gordon, who had passed up a morning of fishing with Sam, watched from the back of the courtroom, then slipped out and strolled through town to Harperville's lone florist. With uncharacteristic hesitation, he considered a variety of arrangements before choosing one he thought would be appropriate to take to Ellen.

It was a cool morning, and the wind coming from the northwest had a bite that signaled the changing of the seasons. Gordon drove the bouquet back to Twin Creek Ranch, and as he arrived, he wondered if he was only imagining a stillness and somberness hanging over it, like the billowy white clouds that from time to time obscured the view of the sun.

Ellen came to the door herself, and Gordon could tell from the involuntary sparkle in her eye and upward turn of the corners of her mouth that she liked the flowers. She set them on a coffee table between a large sofa and the hearth, in which a good fire was burning. He accepted her offer to stay for a cup of coffee.

"It was sweet of you to do this," she said, admiring one of the blossoms.

He shrugged.

"You left really early this morning and missed all the excitement."

"Excitement?"

She nodded. "I've calmed down a bit now, but I was really shaken when it happened. About seven o'clock this morning, after I'd gotten up and showered, I came into the kitchen to make coffee like I always do. This girl needs her coffee, so I was still half asleep, but when I finally got a cup ready, I went over to sit down at the kitchen table. When I pulled out one of the chairs, I heard a rattling noise. I've heard that noise before, outside, and I knew what it was. I jumped back so fast I must have gone clear across the room. There was a rattlesnake under that table. A big one."

Gordon felt his skin tingling. He didn't care for snakes, and the thought of a dangerous one appearing inside a house was more than unnerving. "But how did it get in?" he asked.

"It happens," she said. "They're around and the doors do get left open. But, God, what a wake-up call."

"What did you do then?"

"What else could I do? I got the poker from the fireplace and came back to the table. Fortunately, the snake was still there …"

"Fortunately?"

"Of course," she said. "If it was gone, that would mean it was somewhere else in the house. Anyway, it was back up against the wall and still coiled, so I pulled the table away to expose it. It decided to run for it, which made things a lot easier. I killed it, but it took three whacks to do it."

"Why didn't you call for help?"

She looked at him like a stern teacher faced with a not-too-bright child. "Whatever on earth for? I've killed rattlesnakes before, and it's not that complicated. You just move fast and do it."

Gordon's mouth was dry and his chest muscles had tightened. For a minute he said nothing, then he took a deep breath and let it out."

"Ellen, are you sure that snake got into this house by itself?"

"What do you mean?"

"There was that bale of hay that fell from your barn door last Friday. Now this. Don't you see a pattern here?"

"The hay was obviously done by somebody," she said. "This is the sort of thing that happens on its own." She sounded as if she was trying to convince herself.

"Can I ask you a question?" She nodded. "Is the house secure at night? Are all the doors and windows locked?"

"Of course not. Nobody does that here."

"So it's possible that someone could have opened a door or window and put that snake in the house."

"It's possible, but I really don't think that's what happened."

"Listen, Ellen, some time in the middle of the night I thought I heard a car engine outside. I looked and couldn't see anything, but I'm really wondering now."

Her face clouded over. "Some time in the middle of the night I woke up because I thought I heard a strange noise. It could have been a windowsill going down or a door closing, but when I didn't hear anything else after a while, I went back to sleep."

They looked at each other for a moment. Then there was a knock on the door and one of the ranch hands stepped into the house.

"Excuse me, Ellen, but I wanted to let you know we put that snake on the trash fire a few minutes ago. He'll be cremated pretty soon."

She nodded her head. "Thank you, Dennis."

"Before we did, we laid him out and measured him. He was four feet, five inches long exactly."

For a moment, Gordon was merely awed by the size of the snake, but then he began to do some mental arithmetic, remembering what Hart Lee Bowen had said to him on the West Buchanan Friday morning.

"I like to go after them with a stick and a loop myself. I caught four the day before yesterday. One of them was fifty three inches long."

Gordon turned to Ellen. "Call the sheriff," he said.

• • •

"It's been interesting," said Ellen. "This is a situation that strains the bounds of traditional etiquette. How do you respond to a death in the family, when the one who died was suing the rest of the family and got shot in cold blood?"

Gordon shrugged. They had sat down with coffee after she had called the sheriff. Baca had asked a few questions and said he'd keep the incident on file. That was as much as could be expected. After the call, Ellen was eager to change the subject and Gordon, too, was happy to put it aside for the moment.

"Most of the town seems to be stumped, too. A lot of our friends haven't called, and I'd like to think it's because they don't know what to say. I don't altogether blame them. And some of the people who have called said the most amazing things. Mrs. Morgan at the feed store actually said, 'It's awful what happened to poor Dan,' then she lowered her voice and almost whispered, 'But maybe it's for the best after all. And Mary Ann Snyder, who's known me forever, asked if it was true that Dan shot himself because he had AIDS and didn't want to face it."

"You're joking."

"I can see you don't know what it's like living in a small town. Everybody thinks everybody else's business is their own. I'm sure Mary Ann had no idea she was asking a question that a lot of people would have found offensive."

"Didn't *you* find it offensive?"

"Not really, because I know her and know where she's coming from. To her, that was no different than asking if someone's cold was getting better. You know, as much as all this is getting to me, I'm getting a perverse pleasure out of these comments. I'm even wondering who's going to come up with the grand champion."

"You're handling it a lot better than I would."

"What I don't like, though, is people thinking that I wanted Dan dead because of the lawsuit. He's my brother, for God's sake. I didn't want him to die — just leave us alone and honor dad's wishes. Even Sheriff Mike was looking at me funny last night and asking some insinuating questions."

"Ellen, have you talked to an attorney?"

"Why should I do that?"

"It might not be a bad idea."

"It is a bad idea. I haven't committed a crime or done anything wrong. Therefore, I don't need a lawyer. It's that simple."

"I believe you, but you're not thinking straight about the rest of it. My father's a judge, and he always said it's foolish for someone under suspicion to talk to the police alone. Sometimes you say something you don't mean to say and it hurts you or throws the investigation off course."

"So I'm under suspicion, am I? Well, it's not surprising, considering the trial and the missing gun, and the fact I don't have an alibi. But I didn't do it, and I don't have anything to hide, and I trust Sheriff Mike to be fair. So thanks for the advice, but no deal."

"What do you think happened to the gun?"

"I have a pretty good idea. Dan was by the house several times in the last few weeks. I think he probably took it and didn't bother telling me."

"Would he do that?"

"Why not? It was his gun."

"Did you tell Baca about that?"

"Of course I did. He's probably looking into it."

"Do you have any idea when it disappeared?"

She shrugged. "The gun case is just another piece of furniture in this house. I walk past it so many times every day I don't pay attention to it. And Dan's gun was at the end of the row, so it wouldn't have been as noticeable as if it was missing from the middle."

"Can you remember the last time you were conscious of seeing it?"

"Sure. Two weeks after dad's funeral I made up a list of all the things in the house I thought were Dan's, plus a few personal effects mom and dad might have liked him to have. The gun was on the list I sent him. Funny, a week later I got the notice that the will was being challenged. Anyway, a week before the trial started, when I knew Dan would be coming up here, I took that rifle out of the gun case and cleaned it in case he asked for it. That's the last time I consciously saw it."

"That narrows it down a bit." Gordon set down his empty coffee cup. "Thanks for the coffee. And I'm sorry you're having to go through all this."

"Don't feel sorry for me. Please. Anything but that."

"I didn't mean ..."

"No, I know you didn't. It's just that I have to get through this in my own way, and I'll do it. I don't need pity, but companionship is welcome, so if you'd like to come by and talk some time, I'll be glad to see you." She paused. "And thank you for saying you believe me."

• • •

He met Sam for lunch at Mom's Cafe and learned that the East Buchanan had cleared and fishing had been good that morning. Sam had caught and released five trout, including a 15-inch rainbow, and was in the best of spirits. Gordon agreed to return to the river in the afternoon, but not until he had talked with Baca first.

"It's possible her brother made off with the gun and somebody at Radio's camp has it," he said. "From what little I know of that bunch, it seems more than likely."

"And it seems more than likely to me that the sheriff is probably considering that possibility among others," Sam said. "You know, Gordon, you were a lot more fun when you were trying to be a fisherman instead of a detective."

"Knock it off, Sam. I have a stake in this. After all, I discovered the body. I've never found a dead body on a fishing trip before."

"Poor guy," said Kitty, interrupting the conversation as she brought their food. "It couldn't have been pleasant. A thirty ought six would make a real mess out of a man."

"It was bad enough," Gordon agreed. He lowered his voice, "Tell me, Kitty, are people talking about it?"

"Are you crazy? Of course they are."

"What seems to be the ... the general feeling about it?"

"Not good. I'd say about two thirds of the people who have an opinion think Ellen did it."

"What do you think?"

"I *know* she didn't do it. There's no way I can prove it, but I know" She paused. "What do you think about that rattlesnake this morning?

"What do you think?"

"Excuse me," said Sam. "What's this about a snake? Is there something I should know about?"

Gordon briefly recounted the story, and Sam whistled when it was over. "If they have rattlesnakes that big crawling into houses," Sam said, "I think we should move our base of operations into town."

Kitty laughed. "There's rattlers everywhere in this county," she said. "But you've got to get in their face and insult them real bad before they'll bite you, so just be careful. They were probably all over the place when you boys were fishing below the ranch house yesterday."

"I never saw any," said Sam.

"Doesn't matter," Kitty said, "They saw you."

"So what do you think, Kitty," said Gordon. "Did that one just crawl into the house on its own?"

Her eyes darkened. "I doubt it. That snake didn't get to be that big and old by making mistakes like this." Gordon nodded. "How's Ellen doing today?"

"I'd say she's tired but feisty. All of this has to be wearing her down, but she's trying not to let it."

"Poor kid. I think I'll go over after closing and keep her company. And it wouldn't hurt for you to go see her again tomorrow."

"You really think so?"

Kitty topped off his coffee cup. "I really think so," she said.

• • •

"Yes," Baca said, "it had occurred to me that Dan McHenry might have taken that gun. But where does that leave us?"

"It leaves us," Gordon said, "with the distinct possibility that Radio or someone in his camp might have used it to kill Dan McHenry."

Baca smiled. "Maybe you're right. At the moment, there's no hard case against anyone, and if I have to run someone in for this murder, it would please me no end for the responsible party to be Mr. Rex Radio. But I don't think so."

"Why not?"

"What's his motive?"

"He stands to inherit the ranch, for crying out loud."

"He stood a better chance of inheriting it when Dan McHenry was alive and in front of the court as the wronged son. If the case was over and settled, I'd be a lot more inclined to suspect him. But if he killed Dan McHenry, he'd only be making things more complicated for himself, and the man's no fool."

"Maybe something was going on inside that group that we don't know about."

"That's entirely possible. And if I knew for a fact what it was, I'd have something to act on. But I don't."

"Aren't you going to at least look for the gun at Radio's camp?"

"Didn't your daddy teach you anything about the law? I suppose I could go up there and talk with Rex Radio man to man and ask for his permission to search the camp. But do you really think for a minute that he'd do anything but tell me to get the hell out?"

"Couldn't you get a warrant?"

"Let me make this real simple. In order to get a warrant, I have to show probable cause to believe that what I want to search for will be there. The local judge is hardly a bleeding heart, and he has more faith in me than I have in myself. But if I go into his court and tell him I want to search a campsite because somebody who might have been there might have taken a gun from the McHenry house at some unspecified time during the last six months — even though nobody saw him do it — well, I'd get a horse laugh and no warrant."

"So are you just going to do nothing?"

"Hardly. We have a crew from our posse searching both sides of the road from the McHenry ranch to town, looking for the murder weapon. They should cover two miles a day and be done by sundown Wednesday."

"If they don't find it, does it look better for Ellen?"

"Maybe a little. But it advances the case a lot more if they find something."

"How much more would you need to arrest her?"

Baca leaned back in his chair and deliberately lit a cigarette, blowing out a big plume of smoke. "You know, Gordon, I thought you were here on a fishing trip."

"All right. I can take a hint."

"To answer your question, in a general sort of way, what I need to make an arrest in this case — or any other — is enough evidence to satisfy myself that I'm doing the right thing and to satisfy a judge at a preliminary hearing to certify the case to superior court for trial. What that amounts to varies from case to case."

"Point diplomatically made. Now if I can change the subject, what do you think about the rattlesnake in the McHenry kitchen this morning?"

Baca took a drag on his cigarette and lazily blew out three perfect smoke rings. "I'd say at least once a year somebody in this county finds a rattlesnake in their house. And those are just the cases I hear about."

"So you don't think it's suspicious."

"Don't get impatient, now. Let me finish. Usually it happens in the spring, when they've come out of hibernation, and usually the snake involved is two feet long or less. So yes, I think it's suspicious, but proving anything is going to be impossible."

"It's an awful way to try to kill someone."

"You don't want to be bitten by a rattlesnake," said Baca. "Take my word for it. It's extremely unpleasant. But hardly anybody dies from it these days. If it is what you think, it was probably more an act of terror than a serious attempt at murder. It's going to be a long time before she feels comfortable in her own house again."

Gordon got up. "You're probably right, and that just makes it worse."

"Listen," said Baca, "you did a very good job of handling the situation with the finding of the body and answering questions. You'll make a great witness, if it comes to that, and I appreciate it. And if you should come across any hard evidence, as opposed to speculation, come by the office any time or call me at home. I'll be glad to hear it and act on it. But don't go running around trying to solve the case. Do we have an understanding?"

"I'll tell you tomorrow," Gordon said. "Right now, I'm going fishing."

• • •

The first thing Gordon did when he and Sam reached the Sportsman that night was to take a discreet look into the bar. Radio, Bowen, and Horton were at their customary table in the corner. After placing his dinner order, Gordon told the waitress to take them a round of drinks. Several minutes later, Radio came by, holding a bourbon and water. There was a slight unsteadiness and hesitancy in his speech that showed the drink wasn't his first. He took an empty chair at their table for four.

"Thank you for your munificence," he said. "To what do I owe the pleasure?"

"Don't mention it," said Gordon. "I've had two rounds on you, so it's my turn. Besides, I was wondering if you heard what happened to Ellen McHenry this morning."

"Can't say as I have."

"When she went into the kitchen this morning, there was a rattlesnake under the kitchen table. It almost bit her before she saw it."

Radio pursed his lips and took a deep breath. "My, my, my, my, my," he said on the exhale. "That would have been unfortunate." He took a sip of his drink. "What happened to the snake?"

"She killed it with a fireplace poker," said Sam.

"I'm not surprised. She's not the type to show mercy."

"It did get me to thinking," said Gordon, "that your friend Hart Lee was catching rattlesnakes up where you're camped."

"A good man, Hart Lee. Herpetology is only one of his many and varied interests."

"I don't suppose one of them might have found its way to the McHenry Ranch, now?

Radio laughed. "I'm shocked, Gordon. That's a wild supposition without an iota of fact to back it up."

"You're good at rhetoric, anyway."

"Used to make a living at it. Can't do that any more, though. Have to be politically correct, and I'm not."

"Neither is Rush Limbaugh, and he was making a living at it the last time I looked."

"If he was in San Francisco, they'd throw him off the air, too. Only reason they don't now is he's national. It'd be bad PR."

"Maybe. I'm afraid I don't see it that way."

"That's 'cause you have a job. You never got fired for speaking the truth." Radio took a nip of his bourbon and gave Gordon a hard stare. "Let me ask you gentlemen a question. Do you believe in the Second Amendment?"

"I do," said Sam after a brief pause. "But unlike a lot of people, I like to read it in its entirety, beginning with the words, 'A well regulated militia ...'"

"See, that's where you damn liberals don't get it. Militia, militia, militia. What's a militia anyway except the sovereign people who've taken up arms to protect themselves against the government?"

"But isn't a militia supposed to enforce lawful authority?" Sam asked.

"What's lawful authority when the government's corrupt itself? They can't balance their budget, so they print paper money without gold to back it up; and they tax the people who produce to support the people who don't. Only an uprising of armed citizens can stop that. The country's just waiting for someone who has the guts to get it started."

"Does that mean this is the place and you're the man?" asked Gordon.

"This is as good a place as any. Better, maybe."

"Why here?"

"Because there are still some real Americans here who believe in the things that made this country great. 'Cause this place hasn't been overrun by the vermin that have taken over San Francisco and all the other big cities. And there's one more thing."

He paused, and Gordon and Sam could only look on in mute discomfort.

"Gold. People don't realize it, but there's still gold in these mountains. And that's going to be important. You know why?"

Gordon said he didn't.

"I'll tell you why. The world order that's been created by the Reds and the Trilateral Commission and the Freemasons is going to collapse. The dark ages are coming, and when they do, this funny money we carry around ain't gonna be worth squat. Only one thing will be universal currency, and that's what it's always been. Gold. Even a small place like Summit County can be a self-contained fortress of enlightenment if it has gold to buy what it needs and buy off those who'd destroy it."

"And a militia to protect itself," Gordon said mockingly.

"Damn right. And a well-regulated militia, Mr. Bleeding Heart Liberal."

"How many guns do you have at your camp, Radio?"

"None of your business. Or the government's."

"What I'm really interested in is one gun in particular."

"I might sell if the price is right."

"I don't want to buy it. I just want to know if it's there. Did Dan McHenry bring back a deer rifle from his house during the last few weeks?"

"How would I know? Everybody in the camp has a gun or two."

"Or three or four."

"Don't be a smartass. Nobody likes a smartass. Besides, last time I looked it was still legal to own more than one gun. I can't pay attention to 'em all."

"This could be important. That could be the gun that killed Dan McHenry."

"Then it isn't in my camp unless his sister sneaked up in the middle of the night and put it there."

"But what if it is?"

"It isn't. Look, kid, I kind of get the feeling you're taking an interest in Ellen McHenry, and that's none of my business. No accounting for taste, but it's none of my business. And if she killed her brother, which she did, you won't find me lifting a finger to help her." He downed the last of his bourbon and got to his feet. "Thanks for the drink, anyway, and be careful. Deer hunting season is on through next weekend." Radio pointed his forefinger at Gordon like a gun, then made a cocking motion with his thumb and a clicking sound with his mouth. He laughed when Gordon flinched involuntarily, then he walked away.

"What a delightful character," said Sam after a long silence.

"A real sweetheart. But I don't believe him about the gun."

"I think you're wearing me down, Gordon. I'm starting to agree with you."

"I wish the sheriff would."

"You know, I can't remember. Radio got fired for saying something pretty bad. What was it?"

The waitress brought their steaks, and Gordon waited until she had gone and they were alone before replying. Even then, he leaned over and spoke softly.

"He was fired," he said, "when Louis Farrakhan was making anti-Semitic comments while Jesse Jackson was running for president. And Radio actually said, on the air, 'Maybe we ought to let the Jews and jigs kill each other off and leave the country for the real Americans.' I'd say he's putting a pretty fine gloss on it when he calls that nothing more than being politically incorrect."

Tuesday September 14

Seven miles south of Harperville the state highway veers to the left, crosses a relatively low mountain pass, and makes its way into Nevada. Forking off the highway, a paved county road follows the East Buchanan into the mountains for seven more miles before coming to an end in Bountiful Valley, elevation 7,138 feet. At one time the valley sustained a ranch, but the ranch buildings have been converted to a pack station that serves as a base for back-country camping trips. The remainder of the valley is owned by a utility company, which leases it for cattle grazing and allows the public to fish the river.

Most of the valley consists of a long and broad meadow, through which the river — more of a creek this far up — meanders in a series of horseshoe curves. In cooperation with the California Wild Trout Project, the utility company several years ago donated materials to build protective fences to keep the cattle away from the water, except at a few selected areas. This prevents streambed erosion, and the fences, made of rough-cut logs carefully notched together, are both effective and visually pleasing.

Gordon and Sam arrived in the valley shortly after nine o'clock in the morning. There was frost on the ground still, and a distinct chill, which the sun had yet to cut through. At the pack station, horses were being readied for the penultimate trip of the season, but otherwise the two men had the valley to themselves.

They began at the end of the road, and fished their way methodically upstream, leapfrogging each other to fish the next likely spot, each man giving the other the full measure of his own space. Sam fished a dry fly on the water, while Gordon, reasoning that it was too early for the fish to be surface feeding, worked below the surface with a Hare's Ear nymph. When he caught and released three fish to Sam's none in the first half-hour (including a 14-inch rainbow trout), Sam switched his fly and began enjoying some success. By eleven o'clock, the sun had warmed the valley considerably and Gordon and Sam had fished about half the section of water running through it.

Gordon decided it might be time to try a dry fly, so he tied a size 14 Yellow Humpy to the end of his leader and cast it to the moving current where the water rushed by and under an overhanging bank. He put the fly just where he wanted — on the inner edge of the current — and three feet below where it landed, it was clobbered by a trout. The fish was a handsome native brook trout, ten inches long, and Gordon held it lovingly for a few seconds after taking the hook out.

"He take a dry?" asked Sam, who had come over to look.

Gordon nodded, then kissed the fish on top of the head and put it back in the water. "Go tell your grandpa we want to see him," he said as it swam off.

They sat in silence for several minutes on the grass by the side of the river. Gordon seemed lost in thought, and finally put a question to Sam.

"When we were talking to Radio last night, did anything he said strike you in particular?"

"Just about everything. Why?"

"I've been thinking about gold. Do you remember what he said about it?"

"What — that we shouldn't have gone off the gold standard?"

"Partly that, but I was thinking more about something else. Didn't he say that one of the reasons for being in Summit County was that there was still gold in the mountains here?"

"Now that you mention it. He seemed to think it would get him through the new world order or something."

"Exactly. And I wonder if we might not be able to get to the bottom of all this by taking him literally."

"What do you mean?"

"Where is it? Where exactly is the gold? When I talked to Baca at the barbecue a few days ago, he seemed to think the mines here had all been picked clean in the last century."

"Are you saying Radio came across a vein of gold somewhere?"

"Could be. You know, if these characters have been hanging around and exploring this county for half the summer, one of them could have checked out a few of those old mines and noticed something. Or maybe they went up a canyon somewhere and found something."

"So what?" said Sam. "I'm not an expert on mining law, but wouldn't he have to file a claim somewhere to get at it?"

"Maybe, but I have another idea. There's apparently an abandoned mine on the McHenry ranch. Baca said so. From his description of where it was, it sounds as if almost anybody could probably get to it without being seen. What if Radio or one of his men did that, and found a gold deposit nobody knew was there?"

"So if you own the McHenry ranch you owned the gold, too?"

"Or if you don't, who'd stop you from mining, if you were discreet. I understand it's fairly isolated. That would definitely add something to the McHenry inheritance." Gordon got to his feet. "Let's fish back to the car and head to town for lunch. I'm sorry to do this to you, Sam, but would you mind fishing alone this afternoon? If Ellen's at home, I'd like to ask her about this."

"Go ahead," said Sam. "I'm getting used to this."

• • •

Thunderclouds were massing over the mountains to the west as Gordon drove across the cattle guard at Twin Creek Ranch shortly before two o'clock. Ellen McHenry was at home, and he laid out his theory over a cup of coffee. She seemed dubious about it, but agreed to show him the abandoned mine. "I was planning on being in court this afternoon," she said, "so all the chores have been assigned to someone else."

The two of them donned parkas in the event of rain and set out across the meadow. She was wearing blue jeans (as was Gordon) and had tied her hair in a bun under her Stetson; anyone seeing them from behind at any distance would have imagined them to be a pair of cowboys heading out to check the cattle.

"It's funny you should make that suggestion," she said as they reached the bend in the creek where Dan McHenry's body had been found. "Whenever the cattle market was rough, which it is about two thirds of the time, Dad always used to say it was too bad that mine was worthless. He said it would have been his salvation from the curse of being a cattleman."

"He didn't mean it, did he — about being a cattleman?"

"Of course not. He griped a lot, because that's what you do when you're in the business and feel like you're always working for the bank. But he wouldn't have done anything else for the world." She paused for a moment. "Neither would I."

They walked in silence for a few minutes more. As they reached the top of the meadow, Gordon noticed a cattle pen and the end of the dirt road that wound along the meadow's back side, the road from which Dan McHenry's killer had presumably fired the fatal shot two mornings ago. He thought to himself that it would be fairly easy to drive up that road unseen and slip up to the mine. Ellen McHenry looked at the road as well.

"You know," she said, "I was just thinking. I haven't been up to that mine in years, but I remember the last time like it was yesterday. It was the Friday before Memorial Day our senior year in high school. Margie Baxter, Pam Gibson, Terry Lee Parmalee and I all squeezed into that little Honda Pam had and drove up the back road after school. Terry Lee had bought two packs of cigarettes from a vending machine and we wanted to smoke them some place where we wouldn't be seen. It was a hot afternoon, and the creek was running high and fast from the snow melt. We had to cross it further up to get to the mine, and the water was so cold. We settled in and for a couple of hours we talked about boys and what we were doing after high school, and just smoked cigarette after cigarette. God, did we feel grown up! Then on the way back, I stepped on a slippery rock as we were crossing the creek and fell right in. It just took my breath away. Like I said, the water was cold, and I came out looking like a drowned rat, and the wind had picked up so I started shaking really bad. I thought we'd never get back to the car. When we did, Pam drove me up to the front of the house and took off laying rubber as soon as I was out of the car."

"Leaving you to face the music by yourself," Gordon said.

"Exactly. At least the water pretty much washed away the smell of the smoke. My mother was all agitated about the way I looked, and I was still shivering pretty badly, and she kept asking how it happened, and I didn't know what to say. About the fourth or fifth time she asked, Dad put his hand on her shoulder very gently and said, 'Liz, maybe we should change the subject and get her dried off.' I was so grateful. That was just like him, too. He understood, somehow, that it was embarrassing but not serious and decided to let it pass."

"You don't smoke any more?"

"No," she said. "I've decided to limit myself to just one vice."

They were following the left fork of Aspen Creek upstream now, walking through a fairly broad and gently contoured canyon, the sides of which were dotted with sagebrush and stray clumps of pines. The creek was five feet wide and less than a foot deep in most places this late in the summer, and it was hard to imagine anyone falling while crossing it or getting particularly wet if they did. A long, rumbling peal of thunder could be heard faintly in the distance. Gordon tried to revive the conversation.

"Where are they now, your three friends?"

"They've all moved on. Terry Lee looked like she might stay. She married her high school sweetheart, whose father owns the feed store, the year after we graduated and had two kids by her fourth wedding anniversary. By the fifth anniversary, she was filing for divorce. He drank and hit her. Three years ago she married the financial officer at the hospital. He doesn't hit her and he doesn't drink; in fact he's so pious he doesn't have any vices at all. I can't stand him. They moved to Reno last year when he got a job at a hospital there.

"Margie went to college at Fresno State, dropped out for a while, and got a nursing degree. She married a doctor she met at a hospital in Marin County, and they're living with their two perfect children in a huge house in Tiburon with matching Beemers in the garage. Every year at Christmas I get a 'Dear Friends' letter telling me about their latest trip to Europe and how they're wondering about whether or not they should send Taylor and Jessica to private school. She won't come to Summit County at all, and her parents have to go to their place if they want to see the grandkids, who, by the way, are holy terrors because they have too many toys and their parents never draw the line for anything.

"Pam's the only one I really stay in touch with. She's living in the LA area and has a pretty good job as a personnel manager for a department store. No luck with men, though. After several disastrous affairs, she finally got involved with a naval officer who was stationed in Long Beach. They went together for three years and finally got engaged just as he got transferred to the Philippines. A month before the wedding, right after the invitations had been mailed out, he stopped calling her, which he used to do several times a week. Ten days passed without a phone call, and then, two weeks before the wedding, she got a letter from Luzon. It seems he'd gotten a local girl pregnant and wound up being the groom at a shotgun wedding. That was a year and a half ago, and she's just now starting to recover. Here's the mine."

They stopped walking. At first Gordon didn't see it. The ground rose gently from the creek to a point about 15 feet above it, then abruptly changed to a steep and rocky slope. The mine shaft entrance was carved into the mountainside at that juncture and offset at an angle where a small gully drained to the creek during snowmelt and after a storm. From where they stood, a solitary pine tree, tilting at a slight angle, partially blocked the view of the opening.

"Let's go," said Gordon.

"What are we looking for, again?"

"I don't know, really. I think just a sign that somebody's been here lately."

A peal of thunder sounded fairly close by as they walked up the grade to the entrance. When they reached it, they brandished the flashlights they had brought, and Ellen moved quickly in front of Gordon.

"Let me go first. I know the way."

They entered a narrow passageway that was dark, cool and musty. It was propped up by timbers that looked old and none too steady. The beams from their flashlights caught the glint of a trickle of water dripping down the left-hand wall.

"That seepage wasn't here the last time," she said. "Over time, that'll soften the earth and lead to a collapse."

"Are you sure this is safe?" Gordon asked. The claustrophobic passage was making him anxious.

"No such thing as a completely safe mine," she replied. "But we're probably OK for now."

"Good."

"Unless there's an earthquake, of course."

"Of course."

"If we go down about 60 feet this'll widen out a bit and there's sort of a natural room that was carved out where they needed some room to maneuver. I wonder if those cigarettes we smoked are still there."

They moved ahead down the shaft. Its ceiling was less than six feet above the ground, so Gordon had to stoop uncomfortably as he walked. It seemed like an eternity before the passageway widened and the ceiling rose about a foot, enabling him to stand up straight. The additional space was a relief, but it also soaked up light. Their flashlights could do no more than open a narrow seam in the darkness, but as they played the beams around the space, they could see that it was filled with boxes of various sorts and was clearly being used as a storage area.

"Good night," said Gordon.

"This wasn't here the last time," Ellen said.

"What is all this stuff?" Gordon moved closer and began playing his light over them at close range. He looked at several without seeing anything, then noticed a label on the side of one.

"Dynamite," he said.

Ellen was checking boxes at the other end of the space and at about the same time said, "Here's a box of ammunition, but what's in these wooden boxes with no markings?"

"Good question. They seem to be nailed shut." He walked slowly among the boxes, playing the light carefully over each. "Hold it! Looks like this one's been opened." The top to that box wasn't nailed down tightly and there was a small space where he could gain purchase with his fingers. Ellen had moved over and was pointing her flashlight at it, so Gordon put his flashlight in a jeans pocket and pulled up on the box lid with both hands. The small nails in soft wood gave way, and he lifted the top open. What he saw inside froze his blood.

"Those," said Ellen McHenry after a long silence, "are no deer rifles."

"I've never seen anything like this outside a movie, but they're obviously some kind of assault weapons." He brought down the lid and pushed the nails back into place.

"This explains so much," Ellen said. "The times Dan wanted to go fishing at the ranch. He must have been keeping watch while they brought this stuff up. What should we do?"

Gordon pushed down the top of the box. "Tell Baca. He mentioned a few days ago that the Alcohol, Tobacco and Firearms people were interested in Radio. I think they'll be even more interested now." He slowly moved the flashlight beam over the chamber. "There must be a hundred boxes of weapons and explosives here. Let's go. This place is giving me the creeps."

They crossed the room to the passageway that led back to daylight. But just as they reached it, they heard a loud crash at the other end, accompanied by cursing. Gordon instinctively reached forward, put his arm around Ellen, and pulled her back to him, but after that he could only stand motionless with fear. The voices picked up again, and she broke from his grip and whispered, "This way."

She led them across the chamber to the passageway on the other side that led farther down into the earth. It was narrower and lower than the one they had come through from outside, and when they had got several feet down it, she grabbed his hand and stopped.

"Kill your light," she said. Then, as they stood in darkness damp and total, she whispered, "I don't know what's down here, so we'd better stop. If we flatten ourselves against the wall, they probably won't see us."

Gordon did as she said. Because of the low ceiling he had to squat slightly and stick his knees out in a wretchedly uncomfortable position. No more than a few seconds later, they could hear the sound of bumping and swearing, gradually drawing nearer. Then a blaze of light, almost blinding, illuminated the underground room full of weapons. Moving with surprising grace, Hart Lee Bowen came in, carrying a lantern ahead of him in his right hand and holding a box like the one full of assault weapons behind him in his left hand. George Horton came in behind him, carrying the other side of the box with both hands. They dropped it on the hard earth from a height of a foot, and the crash it made echoed through the chamber and into the passageway where Gordon and Ellen waited breathlessly, just out of range of the lantern light.

"How many more times are we going to have to do this?" asked George, in an annoyed tone.

"George, do you ever do anything but complain?"

"We need a mule or something to carry this stuff."

"When the boss gets the ranch for keeps, we can run pack horses up here, but until then, we're going to have to do the work ourselves. There's too much chance of being seen as it is."

"Why do we need so many guns? We must have a hundred for everybody in our camp."

"Honest to God, George. Don't you get it yet. It's not just us we have to take care of. We're building a people's posse. When this corrupt society breaks down, other people are going to want to join us, and we have to be ready to be the militia for this county, or whatever part of it is still standing. We'll have to fill this room from floor to ceiling to do that."

There was a pause while the two men breathed heavily from their exertions, then George spoke.

"Hart Lee, do you really think we're going to get the ranch? It somehow doesn't seem right that we should get it without Danny?"

"Of course we will. And don't think twice about it. You know Dan would have wanted it this way. I mean, that's how he made out his will."

"Ah, yes, the will."

"What does that mean?"

"Well, it was a bit of a surprise. I never knew he'd made one out, but if he had, I would have thought after our five years together ... Well, never mind."

"You weren't the only one, you know. There were others."

"Thank you for calling it to my attention," George said acidly. "I know about you and at least some of the others. But still, he always came back to me."

"Anyway, it's better that we get it than his sister. Not that she has a chance. Word is she's going to be arrested for murder any day now."

"That would be too bad. She didn't do it, you know."

"Oh, yeah?" Bowen's voice was taking on an edge of exasperation. "How do you know?"

"I just do. There are some things you know in your bones."

"All I know in my bones is it'll be a lot easier for us if she gets sent up for the killing."

"Wouldn't it be enough for us to get the ranch without that? Why should she suffer any more?"

"George, where were you when Dan was shot?"

"Me?" George seemed flustered. "Why I was driving into town for supplies."

"Do you have any witnesses to that?"

"How could I? I was driving in alone. I usually went with Dan on Sundays, but he was fishing this time, so I went myself."

"Then I wouldn't go around telling people about Ellen McHenry's innocence if I were you. Because if she didn't do it, somebody else did, and you'd be a prime suspect."

"Me?"

"Sure. You don't have an alibi, and you have two motives. You might have been jealous of Dan's fooling around, and you might have thought you'd benefit financially from his death."

"Don't be absurd!" The words exploded from George's mouth in a plaintive shriek.

"You're probably right. I can imagine you thinking about it, but I don't believe you'd actually have the guts to shoot someone in cold blood."

"You're horrible."

"No worse than most, George."

"That's not true. Most people don't collect rattlesnakes, then drop them in the kitchen of a woman's house. Don't you feel bad about that at all, Hart Lee?"

"As a matter of fact, I do." He paused. "It was wrong to let that snake die such a horrible death." He laughed, and the vibration of the sound took on a Mephistophelian quality as it rattled off the walls of the mine. The sound echoed for two seconds after he stopped.

"Let's go," said George. "I need some fresh air."

"Not just yet. I'd like to go down and take a quick look at that vein of gold before we head back."

Bowen picked up the lantern and took a step toward the passageway where Gordon and Ellen were hiding. In a split second, several thoughts flashed across Gordon's mind. He realized that there was no going backward; it occurred to him that though he was about the same size as Bowen, the latter was a few years younger and his football experience in hitting people was probably more germane to the approaching conflict than Gordon's ability to sink a feathery jump shot; and he decided that a surprise lunge at Bowen was probably his best chance for prevailing.

"Hart Lee! No!" George's petulant voice stopped Bowen after two steps. Gordon and Ellen remained just beyond the light thrown by the lantern. "It's going to start raining any minute, and that'll take half an hour. We don't have time."

"What's the matter, George? Afraid of the dark?"

"Stop it. I mean what I just said. I'm sore and tired, and I don't want to get rained on if I don't have to."

"I guess you're right, but I do love to look at that gold. It just makes me feel warm and fuzzy all over to know that the McHenry bitch is sitting on several million dollars worth of it and doesn't have a clue it's there."

"You are not a nice person, Hart Lee."

"And you're too nice for your own good, George. All right. We'll have it your way." He turned around, and the light quickly began to recede from Gordon and Ellen. The chamber went dark abruptly as the two men left it.

Gordon let his breath out and realized he had no idea how long he'd been holding it.

"Are you all right?" she whispered.

"I think the question is are *you* all right?"

"Fine. How long do you think we should wait?"

He broke the darkness by shining the light on his watch. It read three fifteen. "Let's give them fifteen minutes," Gordon said. He was beginning to be acutely conscious of the various aches and pains his awkward position had led to. "I'm glad they didn't come in here. I wasn't looking forward to that fight."

"I don't blame you," she said, "I think I could have handled Bowen all right, but you would have had your hands full with George."

In the dark and stillness it took a few seconds for that remark to sink in, but when he got it, Gordon quickly turned his flashlight on Ellen. Her left hand was over her mouth, and her body was shaking as she tried to suppress her laughter. A surge of nervous release went through his body like an electrical current and he, too, began to laugh uncontrollably, subduing the noise by biting the sleeve of his shirt. His sides ached when he finally stopped several minutes later.

"Point to you," he panted, "but don't do that again. We'd have been dead if they'd come back."

They waited a few minutes more, then he checked his watch again. "Three twenty eight. Close enough. Let's go."

With their flashlights barely penetrating the darkness, Gordon and Ellen crossed the chamber and reached the passageway leading out. He grabbed her as they started out. "Just a minute," he hissed. "There's a chance they might be waiting by the entrance if it's raining. Maybe I'd better go look."

"Stay here," she whispered. "I'm smaller and I know the passage better. I'll do it."

Before he could protest, she was off. He checked his watch and decided to give her ten minutes, then go to her rescue if she wasn't back by then. She was back in nine.

"All clear," she said, "but it's raining cats and dogs. Poor George is getting wet after all." Lights on, they made their way up the passage. As they turned a corner and saw the opening, a flash of lightning illuminated the gray sky visible on the other side of it. A loud thunderclap followed three seconds later, causing a slight reverberation in the tunnel. Gordon shivered as he remembered what she had said about earthquakes when they had first come into the mine. At the entrance, they could see the rain pelting down outside.

"We're probably going to get soaked no matter what," but let's at least wait here until the lightning passes," she said. For the first time in an hour, Gordon got a good look at her. The exposure to danger had left her eyes lively and dancing and her face vital and radiant. He very much wanted to kiss her, but didn't yet feel he had the standing to try. And so, for three quarters of an hour, they watched the rain and talked about the meaning of what they had seen and heard, and how they would explain it to Sheriff Mike Baca.

• • •

Ginger, the receptionist, was on the way out when Gordon reached Baca's office, at half past five..

"Sheriff in?" he asked.

She shook her head. "He just left fifteen minutes ago, but you can find him at the Stage Stop. He has dinner there every Tuesday."

Gordon gave thanks for Baca's regular habits and ran back to his car. The rain had stopped, but the ground was wet and dotted everywhere with large puddles. The sky was still dark, and he turned on the lights as his Cherokee left town.

The Stage Stop is a Summit County institution. Located several miles north of Harperville, it sits at the foot of a pass that connects Summit County with the next county north and is the only connection with California in the winter. Stagecoaches had stopped there in days gone by, but now it provides the setting for a bar and restaurant serving steak and seafood. None but the uninitiated tourist eats the seafood, since the steaks are the best in the county and the fish is frozen.

As he pulled into the gravel parking lot, Gordon spotted a sheriff's car parked near the front door. The lot was half full, so he pulled into the first space he saw and went in. The building was designed to look like a western-movie version of a saloon from the outside, and the interior maintained the general theme, with wormwood walls, cattle-branding equipment, and paintings of cowboy scenes, done in a faux Norman Rockwell style, providing the decor. After entering the front door, he found the bar to his left (through swinging doors, of course). Baca was standing at one end of it, nursing a double Jack Daniels and talking with a local Gordon didn't recognize. Gordon waved to him, then got himself a double scotch and moved down to the sheriff. Beset by impatience, he gripped the glass tightly as Baca introduced him to the other man and engaged in a few minutes of small talk.

Finally, the man left and Gordon muttered under his breath, "I need to talk to you. Major development."

Baca raised his eyebrows almost imperceptibly. "Let's have some dinner," he said. Drinks in hand, they moved out of the bar to the front of the restaurant, where a young woman greeted them. "The corner booth, Nancy," Baca said, "and keep the one next to it open as long as you can."

"Sure thing," she said, with an ease that suggested this wasn't the first time she'd had such a request. They sat down at a table covered with a blood-red cloth and flanked by well-padded black seats, covered by tape in one or two places that wanted repair. After they ordered, Gordon told his story in chronological order, beginning with his dialogue with Radio the previous evening. He finished just as the steaks arrived.

"You know," said Baca, "I ought to give you a badge and swear you in as a deputy. You're coming up with more than any of my men."

"What are you going to do about it?"

"Right now, nothing."

"Nothing?"

"Well, not exactly nothing. I'll send two men out first thing tomorrow morning to take inventory of what's in that mine. And I'll pass it on to ATF. But I think they want to wait to make a move. They're interested not only in what Radio's got, but in where he's getting it."

"What about the snake? Surely you can prosecute that under some law?"

Baca's eyes narrowed to a slit. "Assuming you recalled that conversation exactly — which, by the way, would be remarkable — Bowen never admitted to anything. And any halfway competent defense attorney could coach George so that his recollection of the conversation was that he said most people don't *approve* of dropping snakes in a woman's kitchen. All we can do on that one now is make them uncomfortable, but we'd never get a conviction. And I want to do more than make Radio and his friends merely uncomfortable."

"Well then, what about the murder investigation? You have another suspect now."

"Why do you say that?"

"George. Dan's boyfriend. He was jealous, so that's a motive. And he can't account for his actions at the time of the killing, so he had opportunity. And it wouldn't surprise me if he had Dan McHenry's deer rifle at the camp, which would give him the means to do it."

Baca cut a piece of steak and chewed it slowly, then washed it down with a sip of the coffee he had ordered to replace the bourbon. After that, he sighed.

"If I didn't know you better," he said, "I'd be starting to get offended by now. Do you think I sit around doing nothing all day? We were at Radio's camp until two o'clock Monday morning questioning everybody there, including George Horton. There's nothing you told me about him that I don't already know."

"So you don't think he's a suspect?"

"I didn't say that. He's on the list of possibles, but his motive isn't as strong as others, and there's a big difference between possibly being at the ranch that morning and definitely being at the ranch."

"In other words, you still think Ellen did it."

"I didn't say that, either. If I really thought so, she'd be under arrest now. I'm just trying to sort out the evidence, and right now it sort of points one way, but it's not conclusive. You know, I don't think you appreciate how much restraint I'm showing. Before you got here tonight, two people came up to me at the bar and wanted to know why it was taking so long to make an arrest. I told them what I just told you. There isn't enough evidence — yet. There may never be enough evidence. And I'm not arresting anybody without good evidence, even if it costs me an election."

"I appreciate that," Gordon said soberly. He took a swallow of coffee. "So people really think she did it."

"Not everybody, but quite a few. It's uglier than you think. Nobody has the brass to say it to my face, but there's talk that I'm giving her special treatment. With all that horse manure out there, I don't like getting climbed on by you, too."

"I'm sorry."

"Apology accepted. Just give me credit for trying."

"Fair enough. But let me ask you a question. You talk about evidence — what evidence do you need?"

"It's pretty obvious, isn't it?" Baca said. "The murder weapon. Until we locate the gun that killed Dan McHenry, we'll have a weak case at best. If you have any more miracles up your sleeve, maybe finding that gun can be one of them."

• • •

Gordon realized, as he drove back to the ranch well after nightfall, that he had promised to meet Sam for dinner at the Sportsman three hours earlier, and had completely forgotten about it after the discovery at the mine. Sam had dined alone and had been back at the cabin for more than an hour by the time Gordon arrived. Gordon did his best to be contrite, but his friend would have none of it.

"You could have at least called the Sportsman," Sam said. "Your manners are going to hell, Gordon."

"I'm sorry, Sam, but let me tell you what happened today."

"I'm sure it's a great story. Greatest story in the history of the universe." He sounded a bit tipsy, and this was confirmed when he brought out a half-bottle of cognac and poured a few ounces into an aluminum cup. "Half this could have been yours, Gordon, if you'd been on time. Great thing, punctuality."

Gordon held out his own cup and Sam poured the last three ounces of the bottle into it. He took a gulp, and the alcohol sent a current of fire through his body, warming him against the chill night. "This stuff'll kill you young."

"Yeah, but you'll die happy," said Sam. "All right, let's hear your story."

And for the second time in a few hours, Gordon described what had happened that afternoon, a time that now seemed years removed. Outside, the wind that occasionally rustled the tops of the pines had a cutting edge to it, and the lingering storm clouds kept the sky starless. Gordon was feeling drained by the emotional intensity of the last few days, and the isolated location and weather added a feeling of disconnectedness that further weighed him down. He finished his story and the cognac at the same time, then stared at the cabin wall, spent.

It was a few minutes before Sam spoke. "I have to hand it to you," he said. "We came up here for a week of fishing, and now you've got us in the middle of a

Hitchcock script. I can hardly wait to see what happens next. Too bad we have to go back in a few days."

"I'm not going back."

"What?"

"I'll ask for more time off if I need it. I have it coming. And when this is straightened out, I'll go back just long enough to give decent notice before I quit my job."

"You've threatened to do that before."

"This isn't a threat. Howell, Burns & Bledsoe got along without me for 75 years, they can do it from now on, too. I've made my fortune, and it's time to move on. I can do anything I want, and I intend to take my time figuring out what that's going to be."

There was a long pause. "Well," said Sam, "I wish you luck."

"Thanks."

The two old friends stared silently at the cabin walls and listened to the wind for a few moments, feeling no need to speak. Then Sam suddenly sprang to attention.

"I almost forgot!" he exclaimed. "We got so caught up in your story I didn't get to tell you about my excitement."

"Well?"

"You missed something by not being at the Sportsman tonight. Radio and four or five of his boys were in the bar at the usual corner, and a couple of cowboys from the McHenry ranch came in. The atmosphere was a bit chilly, to say the least. Then Hart Lee Bowen began needling them about working for a killer, and they reacted with a couple of choice phrases about his ancestry and sexual orientation, and before anybody knew what happened, the whole bar was full of people fighting. It was just like a scene from an old Western. Glassware shattering, bodies flying all over the place."

"Was anybody hurt?"

"Just cuts and bruises and concussions as far as I could tell. I was on my way out when it started, and it was over pretty fast, but I found out one thing for sure. I wouldn't want to be up against Hart Lee in a fistfight. He laid out three people in two minutes. You know, Gordon, I'm glad he didn't find you in that mine this afternoon."

Wednesday September 15

"Are you going to the funeral?" asked Gordon.

"I think I'll pass," said Sam. They were having breakfast at Mom's Cafe on a gray and cheerless morning with a cold wind blowing from the north. Inside, a wood stove in the corner was putting out warmth, and the head of a deceased deer watched over the gingham-covered tables from above the main door. The cafe was three quarters full, mostly from the usual business crowd, and the air was filled with the sound of multiple conversations, the clatter of dishes, and shouted exchanges between waitresses and the cook.

Gordon sipped his coffee. "So we go our own ways today?"

"I guess. Dinner at the Sportsman?"

"I'm up to here with beef right now. How about the Chinese place — Bamboo Garden?"

Sam sighed. "Even when I'm on my own, you're shaping my day."

"We can do something else."

"No, the Bamboo Garden is fine. Just promise me you'll be there by six."

"Promise."

Kitty walked up and cast a sideways glance at Gordon's plate. "A Denver omelet, Gordon. This vacation is broadening your horizons."

He smiled. "Don't worry. I'm in control."

"Everything all right?"

Sam and Gordon assured her the food was fine, then Gordon said, "Will you be at the funeral?"

Kitty's mouth tightened as she nodded. "I really don't want to go. You have no idea how much I don't, but I will. I have to be there for Ellen."

"Do you think there'll be a lot of people?"

"Of course there will. That's the problem. It'll be a spectator sport with Ellen as the star player, and everybody else trying to see how she's holding up. This isn't going to be Harperville's finest hour."

Sam was taken aback. "Would it really be that bad?"

Kitty shrugged. "What else could you expect? It's a small town." A customer brought his check to the cash register, and Kitty excused herself to take care of him.

After a moment of silence, Sam said, "Are you sure you don't want to come fishing with me?"

"No, but thanks. And Sam ..."

"What?"

"Don't fall into the creek today. With this wind, you could turn into an icicle."

• • •

The rotating sign in front of the First National Bank of Summit County said the temperature was 45 degrees as Gordon drove past on the way to Saint Louis Catholic Church, where mass would be said for Dan McHenry. The small parking lot was full, and Gordon had to park a block away. The church, built during the boom in the 1920s, was meant to hold 200 people, an optimistic figure these days, even on Easter Sunday, but it was nearly full as he walked in. He was looking for an empty seat, when a voice hissed behind him and to his right.

"Gordon! Over here."

He turned to see Radio, Bowen and Horton sitting together in the last row. Radio was wearing a gray, pinstripe suit and the other two wore blazers and ties. George's coat was well cut and Bowen's looked a fraction too tight for his muscular body.

"We can make room for one more," Radio said in a stage whisper. "George, move down and let Mr. Gordon in." Horton did so with an expression of distaste, and Gordon squeezed in between him and Radio.

"Thanks," he said perfunctorily. He sat quietly for a moment, and feeling the need to make conversation finally said, "I didn't expect to see so many people here."

"Then you don't understand human nature," Radio said in a low voice. "For the folks in Harperville, this is better entertainment than anything at the movie theater.

They all want to see how the grieving sister carries herself so they can go back and keep up the discussion about whether or not she committed murder." He paused. "Small towns are so delightful, don't you think?"

"Did it ever occur to you, Rex," said Horton, his voice dripping with acid, "that maybe some of these people cared for Dan McHenry and wanted to show it?"

Radio didn't miss a beat. "By all means, George. Human nature isn't entirely predictable. But let's remember that Dan hadn't lived here for years, and he didn't exactly die of old age. No getting around that."

"There's one other thing you forgot to mention," Gordon said.

"And that is?"

"Some of us are here to pay respects to the family."

"Your sense of duty, I'm sure, will be appreciated by the proper individuals."

The mass began precisely at 11 o'clock, with Father John Malone officiating. A small parish like Harperville generally gets either a young priest on the way up or an old one on the way down. Father Malone was of the first category. To compensate for the fact that fewer than a hundred people attended the two masses at the church each Sunday, he threw himself into the secular life of the town with a vengeance. Athletic and handsome in a boyish sort of way, he served as an assistant coach for the high school football team and was an active member of the Rotary Club. But today his presence and voice were entirely devoted to one of the most solemn offices of his chosen profession.

This early in his career he had already mastered the ability to move a service briskly along, while maintaining the proper tone and sense of religious drama. As a result, the music and the rituals of the church combined to impart a feeling of comfort and serenity that Gordon hoped was helping Ellen McHenry. When it was time for the eulogy, the audience rustled and leaned slightly forward to hear better. With dramatic effect, Father Malone looked out over the audience slowly, as if attempting to make eye contact with everyone in attendance. Only after a full half-minute of silently scanning the audience did he begin:

"We are gathered here today to grieve for Daniel McHenry and to show our love and support for his family. As most of you are probably aware, this is the second tragedy the family has experienced in this year alone, and that may provide yet another reason for our joining together here — to try to make sense of it all.

"When a man of Daniel's age is senselessly killed — and whatever the motive may have been, it was a senseless killing, because there is no sensible reason for taking a human life — we wonder whether there was some meaning behind it that we are unable to discern. I believe there always is.

"Every man's death reminds us of our own mortality and should therefore make us value our own lives more and vow to do something positive with them. Daniel's death, at far too young an age, reminds us of our closeness to each other and the need we have for the love of our fellow men. And above all, no death is without reason if only we had the gift to see that reason as it exists in God's eyes.

"It is possible that the death of Daniel has set in motion a course of events, not yet played out, that will enable us to make sense of this tragedy. And it is possible that it is not, and never will be, for us to know the meaning of it. But that, too, is a revelation, because it calls upon us to draw on our reservoir of faith and accept and respect the workings of God's will.

"That will may be that the secular authorities find and punish the killer of Daniel, in which case we will all know the outcome. Or God may have reserved judgment for himself, for this we know as a certainty. The perpetrator of a wicked deed may be able to hide from the law, but there is nowhere to hide from God. We must have faith that one way or another, justice will be done, because in the end, it will be. It always is.

"In the name of the father, the son, and the holy spirit. Amen."

• • •

After the mass there was a wake at the ranch, which was attended by about half the people at the service. Ellen McHenry was wearing a black wool dress with a pearl necklace. The stark simplicity of the outfit showed her features to good effect and accented her femininity. Gordon was struck by the fact that the first time he saw her dressed up should be at a funeral. He wanted to be with her, but saw no way of politely detaching himself from Father Malone, who had heard about Gordon's athletic background and was engaging him in a mostly one-sided conversation about the Harperville High School football team's progress.

No one expected Radio and his entourage to come to the ranch, and when they walked through the front door it had a dramatic impact. One by one, the groups of people scattered around the front room of the house recognized their presence and fell silent. Ellen, who had been talking with Kitty, noticed the hum of background noise subsiding and quickly spotted the new arrivals. She fixed Radio with a steely glare that almost dared him to do something. He responded by locking eyes with her, and for a moment they stood in place as the room grew totally quiet.

The silence was broken by Kitty's voice, which crackled with the hard edge of suppressed anger.

"It's so good of you to stop by," she said. "Who's carrying the rattlesnake today?"

Bowen's face turned crimson all the way to the roots of his hair. Radio looked quickly at the ground, looked up again, and walked over to Ellen and Kitty.

"I didn't know if I should come by," he said, "but it seems to me if there's ever a time to put differences aside, this is it. We feel the loss of Dan very keenly, and I know you do, too. Let's at least understand we have that in common."

Whether he meant it or not, the sentiment was so irreproachable (and so beautifully delivered in that famous velvet voice) that a harsh response was impossible. The corners of her mouth moved briefly upward in a hint of a smile, then she replied. "Thank you. That's very kind."

At that point the room was utterly silent, and Radio walked over to Gordon and Malone. "Father," he said, "I don't know if anybody's told you this, but that was a first-rate eulogy." With his theatrical sense for the grand gesture, Radio had improbably brought the situation back to a semblance of normality, and within a minute the buzz of conversation was going again. Father Malone soon moved off, leaving Gordon and Radio by themselves.

"You know," said Radio, "I'm having to change my opinion of that girl. She looks really good in that dress. You should take her to San Francisco with you. I'll bet life in the city would suit her just fine. There'd be a lot more to do than around this place. Really, I don't know why she wants to stay here."

"Maybe it's her home. Did that ever occur to you?"

"I guess that's it. May not matter anyway, if she's headed to jail."

The barb got under Gordon's skin, and he decided to jab back. "I wouldn't bet the ranch on that, if you'll pardon the expression. She's not the only suspect."

"Oh, really? I thought you'd ruled me out."

"There's somebody else who had both a motive and the opportunity to commit the crime. Somebody in your group." He lowered his voice to a conspiratorial whisper. "George Horton."

Radio laughed. "You can't be serious. Why George's heart breaks whenever he has to swat a fly at the dinner table."

"Would I make something like this up? Look, Radio, it's common knowledge that George was jealous of Dan

McHenry and his flirtations. That may not seem like much, but jealousy has killed a lot of people in the past. And he can't account for where he was at the time of the killing. He says he was headed into town, but nobody can vouch for his being there until well after the crime was committed. And I'd presume that with all the target practice you folks have been taking up at Sullivan Meadows, old George must be a pretty good shot. In fact, I'd bet that Dan McHenry standing by himself by the creek at this ranch looked just like those silhouettes of the Clintons you were shooting at last week."

"Don't get smarmy about those targets," Radio snapped. "You can't make anything out of that."

"No offense intended," Gordon said. He enjoyed knowing that he had irritated Radio, and hoped that he'd planted a seed of suspicion as well. "I was just trying to tell you how it might look to the law."

"If the law really believed that, they'd have been on us like flies on manure. The sheriff is just looking for an excuse to jump on us. But he can't do it, because we're a lawful militia with no aim but self-defense."

"Whatever you say." He paused and put a tinge of sarcasm into his parting words. "Nice talking to you."

As he turned his back to Radio and walked across the room toward Ellen, Gordon allowed himself to break a smile.

"What were you doing talking to him?" she asked.

"Nothing much," he replied. "Just trying to stir things up a little."

• • •

"I need to get away from here," Ellen said a few minutes later.

"Let me take you to dinner," Gordon offered.

"Thanks, but I don't think so. Anywhere around here, I'm afraid I'd be the center of attention, and that wouldn't make for a fun evening. For either of us."

"Poor thing. You're almost a prisoner in your own home."

"Don't feel sorry for me, damn it."

"All right. Don't be so touchy."

She was silent for a moment. "I have an idea, if you're willing. Have you ever been to Costello Camp?"

"I don't think so."

"It's our high country cattle camp. We could drive up there and I could fix dinner. It would get me away from here for a couple of hours. And you've been so helpful I'd like to do something for you."

"Well ..."

"Do you like beef stir-fry?"

"All right. You're on. Want me to drive?"

"That would be fun. I'd like to see what a Cherokee is like."

"Oh, come on. Around here?"

"Sure you see a lot of them, but they're all driven by tourists who wouldn't dream of putting hay in the back. It's a city macho vehicle, but I still want to see what it's like."

• • •

Not long afterward, Gordon looked out the window and saw George Horton sitting by himself in the deserted, windswept picnic grove. It occurred to him that this might be a good opportunity to pick up information, so he got a cup of coffee to fortify himself against the cold and went outside.

"Mind if I join you?"

Horton looked up. There was a sadness in his eyes and his voice, when he spoke, had the tempo of a record being played just a little too slow. "If you'd like to," he said. "I came out here to think, but I'm about out of ideas."

It struck Gordon in an instant that he had been too blind to realize that Horton must be feeling a pain that could only be deepened by the fact that it occurred outside a societal context that most people could appreciate. Gordon himself, a tolerant man who had certainly been exposed to the gay culture in San Francisco, hadn't really been thinking of George as the surviving, grieving lover he was.

"This has to be hard for you," Gordon said quietly. "Dan McHenry must have meant a lot to you, and now ..." he stopped, not knowing what to say next, and wondering if he had said too much already. Horton looked at him for a few seconds.

"Thanks," he said. "I think you're the first person who's realized that." He shook his head. "You know, I was probably one of two people in the church today who was genuinely sad that Dan was gone. Out of all those people."

"Who was the other one?"

"His sister, of course. They may have been fighting with each other, but there was a feeling there. I could see it."

"Even after the will? The lawsuit?"

"Have you ever really loved somebody, Mr. Gordon? I mean loved them so much you put them ahead of yourself and allowed them to walk all over you and break your heart?" Gordon hadn't, but before he could answer, Horton continued. "It's like the way some mothers love their children, so much they can't stand up to them and the kids turn out to be no good. I loved Dan that way, and he cheated on me and made fun of me behind my back because he knew I'd always be there for him. There were times I could have killed him, and sooner or later we'd have gone our own ways. Not because I would have wanted to, but because he would have found someone else and kicked me out of his life. Do you think it's better it ended like this — I mean, from the standpoint of the relationship — or would it have been better if it played itself out to the end?"

"I don't know," Gordon said after a moment. "I had a history teacher in high school who once said that you can't assume that because what happened was a disaster, what *didn't* happen would therefore have been better. The alternative may have been worse, and his point was that you'll never know and can't assume anything. I guess my approach to things is to deal with what is, and not with what might have been."

"Maybe that's the way to do it. But I was starting to say about his sister. She may have been fighting with Dan, but she loved him. And I don't think she manipulated her father into changing his will. To tell you the truth, I don't think Dan even believed that."

"Does Radio know you feel that way?"

"I'm sure he suspects. He doesn't like me, but then I don't have to tell you that. I honestly don't know what I'm doing with these people now. I fell in with them because Dan did, but they're living in their own world, and with Dan gone, it has little to do with mine." He paused and lowered his voice. "Don't tell anybody, but I voted for Clinton, for God's sake."

"George! Get your can over here!" Radio's voice bellowed out from near the house. "We need to head back."

"It's all right," Gordon said. "I won't tell him."

Horton smiled and extended his hand, which Gordon shook. "I appreciate your coming out here." Then he was gone.

Gordon stayed out in the picnic area for half an hour, watching the last of the mourners leave and turning over in his mind the conversation with Horton. Was his pain nothing but grief, or did it encompass a secret guilt, as well? Horton had the chance to commit the crime, he obviously knew about the back road that would have put him in position to do it, and he had a motive. He'd admitted as much. *There were times I could have killed him.* It didn't seem entirely credible, but if Ellen McHenry hadn't killed her brother, George Horton had to be the prime suspect.

• • •

It was about four thirty when Gordon and Ellen, changed from their funeral clothes into jeans and flannels, left the ranch, bearing an ice chest full of beef and vegetables and a bottle of Pinot Noir. It was still cold and windy, but the cloud cover was breaking up and from time to time the sun partially broke through and cast a spotlight on a section of landscape.

The dirt road leading to Costello Meadows leaves the state highway a few miles the other side of Harperville from Twin Creek Ranch. Gordon had passed it many times, but since the stream it followed was too small to offer much in the way of fishing, he had never explored it. The path wound its way steeply into the mountains, climbing two thousand feet in nine miles. As if by agreement, he and Ellen avoided talking about the funeral or the lawsuit and mostly sounded each other out on matters of personal history and preferences. He noted with satisfaction that she expressed a mild curiosity about his romantic history. He hated talking about it, but knew from experience that the questions at least meant she was probably interested in him.

The cattle camp was located at the edge of Costello Meadows, on land the McHenrys leased from the Forest Service. It consisted of two small cabins, where ranch hands could bunk if need be, and a large corral, empty at the moment. Cattle — several hundred head — were fanned out all over the meadow and were wearing bells so they could be easily tracked if they strayed off. Craggy peaks rose sharply on the east side of the meadow, and the aspens that dotted its perimeter were at the peak of color and shimmering in the wind.

Ellen led them to one of the cabins. It was fifteen feet wide and twenty feet long, and to call its interior Spartan would be an understatement. Just inside the door was a small, old, wooden table flanked by three even older chairs. On the other side, spanning the entire narrow wall, was a kitchen area. It consisted of a sink with no running water, a propane stove and just enough counter space for a resourceful chef, with two cupboards built into the wall above. The long wall on one side was decorated with a cheap and faded color print of cowboys sitting around a campfire. A third of the other long wall was occupied by a large fireplace, framed in river rock. Several oil lamps and a box of matches sat on its mantel. Foam pads and a pile of blankets were pushed against the opposite wall, awaiting use by the next cowboys who needed to use the cabin for the night.

"I feel better already," Ellen said. "It was a good idea to get away from the ranch."

"Is there anything I can do to help?" Gordon asked.

"Two things." She took a saucepan and handed it to him. "Take this down to the creek and get some water to boil the rice in."

"And?"

"When you're done with that, bring in some firewood and start a fire. It's cold in here."

As he walked toward the creek, the sun was barely above the mountains to the west. It was a quarter to six, and the fading light and cold wind were a bracing reminder that summer was almost over. The creek was three feet wide, clear and icy cold. He knelt on the grass beside it and dipped the saucepan in several times, taking the water out and pouring it back in before finally filling the vessel for good.

He gave the water to Ellen and set to building a fire. There was an ample supply of dry pine logs by the cabin, and he carried in several baskets of wood. Working with smaller sticks, he built a latticework pattern of kindling over crumpled newspapers, then added a larger log at an angle on the top. He thought the flames should flicker up from the paper and catch the kindling well enough. He fervently hoped so, in fact, because few things are more embarrassing to a man than being unable to start a fire with a woman watching.

The fire caught immediately; a quarter-hour after he'd lighted it, Gordon added two logs and felt he could take a break. At the stove, Ellen was stir-frying strips of sirloin in ginger oil with carrots, green peppers, zucchini and mushrooms. The Pinot Noir had been opened and a tin cup containing some was on the counter within her reach. As he walked up, she took another cup out of the cupboard and set it on the counter.

"Help yourself to the wine," she said.

"I see you've already started."

"Ranch rules. Chef gets first dibs."

He poured half a cup. It was an expensive label and worth the price, crisp but complex, with a hint of blackberry and a strong finish.

"This is good," he said. "Can I do anything to help?"

"Just keep an eye on the fire. Dinner should be ready in a few minutes."

Gordon sat down in one of the chairs, but kept his eyes on Ellen more than on the fire. Between the wine and the warmth of the room, the tension of the day was easing out of his body and the memory of the funeral and wake were receding from his mind. Fitfully, though, he tried to think over the events of the past few days. It somehow seemed to him that buried in the recesses of his mind was something that might hold the key to the murder of Dan McHenry. But the cheerfully domestic nature of the setting he occupied made it difficult to focus.

"This is a cozy place," he finally said.

"It's not fancy, but you can't beat the location." She sighed. "Dad and Kitty used to use it as base camp for deer hunting, and it's always been where I go when I want to be alone."

"That was something at the house today, the way Kitty went after Radio and his group."

"That's Kitty all over. She's impulsive and she wears her heart on her sleeve." She paused. "She's been like a second mother to me."

"I thought Bowen was going to die of embarrassment. It's not nice to feel that way, I know, but I took a great deal of pleasure in his discomfort."

"That may not have been such a good idea," said Ellen. "It might cause him to turn mean."

"He doesn't need much turning," Gordon said. "Nevertheless, Kitty is quite a woman. She must have led an interesting life.

"Hard is probably a better word. Her husband up and left her when their daughter was three years old, and Kitty had to raise her on her own. It wasn't easy."

"She must be doing all right now, having her own place and all."

Ellen smiled. "She's there from five in the morning until three in the afternoon seven days a week. Then she has to take care of ordering things and keeping records after that. In the winter, when the tourists are gone, the place is never more than half full. If she takes thirty thousand out of it, she's had a good year. It's not easy to get by up here, Gordon."

"I'm beginning to appreciate that."

She looked up from the stove. "I think you do," she said gently, "and I like that. "This is a lonely and incestuous place, but you've tried — and I think you're pushing yourself to do it — you've tried to get inside it a bit. Of all the people who've come up to our place to fish over the years, you're the only one I could say that about."

"So tell me," he said, "if this is a lonely place, does that mean you're lonely, too?"

He could see her body tense and immediately regretted having asked the question. Then she responded — as he would have expected if he had given the matter any thought — in a characteristic way, by getting back to business. She lifted the lid of the pot on the stove and said:

"The rice is done. Dinner's about ready."

The meal was delicious, and they finished the bottle of wine. Afterward, Ellen brewed a pot of strong coffee, and they spread a blanket on the floor in front of the fire and sat, talking. The caffeine picked up Gordon's energy, and brought his mind back to the subject of the murder. He told her about his conversation with George Horton that afternoon.

"He doesn't strike me as a killer," Gordon said, "but then how many killers do I know?"

"Don't you think it had to be somebody in that gang?"

"Bowen, I'd believe. Radio, too. Either of them would slit somebody's throat for a nickel. Or less if they had a good reason. But they both have an alibi."

"That's an interesting point, though. Dan's throat wasn't slit. He was killed at long distance by someone with a rifle and a telescopic sight. There was something remote about it. If George Horton was going to kill somebody, doesn't that seem like the way he'd do it?"

"You may be right. Anyway, I've planted that seed of suspicion in Radio's mind, and maybe that'll make something happen. It's so frustrating to be caught up in this and feel there's almost nothing I can do about it."

"But you've helped a lot already. Just by thinking to look in that mine, you gave the sheriff a reason to consider someone else but me as a suspect."

"I suppose." He laughed. "This is the strangest fishing trip I've ever been on in my life." He finished his cup of coffee and set it down. The two logs now on the grate were almost burned through and were glowing orange, giving off very little flame. Ellen was lying on her side on the blanket, looking into the fireplace.

"It's getting late," he said. "Shouldn't we be heading back?"

"Whatever on earth for?" she asked softly.

He looked at her for a moment, then got up, put his coffee cup on the mantel, and carefully placed two more logs on the fire. Going back to the blanket, he sat next to Ellen and leaned over to kiss her. She put her arms around him and pulled him down. Outside, a gust of wind shook the trees, and the cattle continued to roam through the meadow, the cacophony of their bells providing music that would last all night long.

Thursday September 16

Gordon got up in the middle of the night and stepped outside to find that the wind had died down and the clouds had cleared. As he looked up into the night sky, a shooting star fired across it, east to west. He vaguely remembered a childhood story about a primitive tribe that believed shooting stars were a portent of a significant occurrence within two days. But it was cold outside and pleasant inside, so he hurried back in and didn't think too much about it.

They were up at first light. As cold as the previous day had been, Gordon was surprised that there was no frost in the meadow, though it was still chilly. He got a fire going, while Ellen fixed coffee, bacon and eggs. Gordon noted that she had brought the bacon and eggs with her in the cooler, which indicated an element of premeditation with regard to the previous evening.

Something had occurred to him as he went to get water for coffee, and he mentioned it as they ate.

"I should have thought of this sooner, but there is one more thing I might be able to do."

"What's that?"

"The gun. That missing deer rifle is at the center of all this. Baca even said as much the night before last. Without the murder weapon he can't make much of a case against anybody. With it, there's an obvious suspect."

"Could it be in the mine?"

"I doubt it. Whoever shot your brother got out of there in a hurry. We know that because Sam and I heard the car go by just a few minutes after the shot was fired. And why make a special trip back to put it in the mine when Radio's camp is full of rifles and it would blend into the scenery?"

"That's not very helpful. Do you think he's just going to let you ransack the camp?"

"Of course not. But if Sam or I can get up there on some pretext or other, we might be able to do a little discreet looking around. Tell me, what does the gun look like?"

"It's your pretty basic deer rifle, a Winchester 30.06, bolt action, and oh!" She put her hand to her mouth.

"What's wrong?"

"Sheriff Mike told me not to tell anyone what caliber the gun was."

"That's all right. He's already told me. Keep going."

"Anyway, it has a bolt action, a six-shot clip, and a Bausch and Lomb 6X scope on the top."

"Does it have any distinguishing marks at all?"

She nodded. "Dan's initials are carved into the left side of the butt, and you couldn't miss them. He got the gun as a birthday present when he was 12 and he was so happy about it that he wanted to mark it right away, so he carved them in with a pocket knife. A block D above a block M. Dad was ready to kill him. He was planning all along to take it back to the sporting goods store and have that done professionally."

"It's something to go on, anyway. Now all I have to do is hope that someone leaves it lying out at camp with the initialed side up."

"Isn't that a pretty remote possibility?"

"We got lucky with your mine," Gordon said. "Maybe lightning will strike twice."

• • •

When Gordon arrived in Harperville at mid-morning, his first stop was at the sheriff's office. Baca looked up from his computer with a knowing smile.

"I won't ask where you were last night, since it's none of my business, but you missed out on the excitement at the ranch." Gordon raised his eyebrows. Baca's smile dissolved into a frown as he continued.

"This is getting serious," he said. "I mean, it's been serious all along, but it's getting worse. Someone tried to incinerate Ellen McHenry last night."

"Good God."

"They might have succeeded, too, except for two things. A., she wasn't sleeping in her room last night," here he paused for dramatic effect and looked at Gordon over the rims of his glasses, "and B, your friend Sam arrived just as the perp was about to act. That probably threw him off just enough to save the house."

"What do you mean?"

"Sam pulled in around ten thirty, and as his pickup was coming up to the house, his headlights hit a man who was standing about ten feet outside the window of the master bedroom. That's where Ellen usually sleeps. The second that happened, the man threw something through the window and ran past Sam's truck to the main gate. There was apparently a vehicle of some sort parked there, and it took off as fast as it could go. Sam decided to stay put and called me."

"Did he get a good look at the man's face?"

"Oh, he was able to identify it beyond a shadow of a doubt. You see, our firebomber was wearing a mask that's been selling pretty well at the local five-and-dime. He was trick-or-treating as Bill Clinton."

Baca paused to let that sink in, then continued. "He was using a crude, but effective molotov cocktail that depended on some holes in the lid for oxygen. The lid was a rotating cover that exposed the holes when you aligned it just so. It appears that the lid was turned to cover the holes, which makes sense, and that when Sam showed up unexpectedly, our man panicked and threw it in without twisting the lid open and giving it any oxygen. If he'd remembered to do that, the house would be a smouldering cinder right now."

They were silent for a moment, then Gordon said, "Did you pay a call on Rex Radio this morning?"

"This morning? Hell, I was up there last night. I wanted to at least interrupt those bastards' sleep. Of course they didn't know anything, and, no, they wouldn't let me look for a Bill Clinton mask, and, oh, the righteous indignation about the unwarranted intrusion into their privacy." He smiled wryly. "Which, technically speaking, I suppose it was. But I wanted to make them sweat a bit."

Baca turned to his computer, punched two keys, and a few seconds later the laser printer near it began whirring. "I have something to show you if I can trust you to keep quiet about it."

"Trust me."

The printer ran off four sheets of paper, which Baca pulled together, stapled, and handed to Gordon.

"This looks like an inventory list for Guns 'R Us," Gordon said, flipping through the sheets.

"That's about right. I had two men in that mine yesterday logging every item into a laptop. As you can see, some of the semiautomatic weapons are missing serial numbers, which, in itself is something to go on. Bill Boyd from ATF is coming by this afternoon to talk about this."

"Are they ready to move now?"

"No, damn it, but they're taking precautionary measures. A team of sharpshooters is flying into Reno tonight, and they have the use of three helicopters if they need them."

"This sounds serious."

"Yeah, well they don't want another Waco."

"Is it that bad?"

"It could be. Radio doesn't have all those guns and explosives in the mine for target practice or dynamiting tree stumps. I'll tell you something else. There's a case of nitroglycerin in that shaft that's old and unstable as can be. It could just about go off if you sneezed too loud. I don't want you or Ellen McHenry going back in there. It's too dangerous."

"Not to worry. You couldn't pay me to go back in that place again. Do you have someone guarding it?"

Baca shook his head. "I may be wrong, but I don't think that's necessary. That stuff's been put in there over a period of time, probably with the idea that they'll win the challenge to the will and take possession. We can look in on it every couple of days or so to make sure it's still there. After all, I have a murder investigation going on, and all my men are pretty busy."

"And how is that investigation going, if I could ask?"

"None of your business," Baca said.

• • •

Gordon swung by Kitty's for an early lunch. It was a bright, sunny day, and already it was getting warm in town. He ordered a hot turkey sandwich with mashed potatoes and gravy, and picked up a copy of The Summit County Echo, the county's weekly paper, which had just come out that morning. The murder of Dan McHenry was the top story, of course, but he held off reading about it until he flipped through the rest of the paper. Before he could get back to the front page, Kitty brought his meal and sat down at the table.

"Do you know where Ellen is?" she asked. "I tried calling her all last night and early this morning, and she wasn't in, and after I heard about what happened last night, I'm really worried."

"You can probably get her there now. She decided after the wake yesterday that she wanted to get away from the ranch, so she went up to Costello Cattle Camp for the night."

Kitty looked at Gordon intently for a few seconds. "I see," she said.

He banged his fork on the plate with irritation. "Don't the people around here have anything better to do with their time than nosing around in everybody else's business? I'm amazed that anybody could have killed Dan McHenry without it being discussed at the grocery store before the killer even got back to town."

She smiled and shrugged. "This is a small town, after all. You don't have to live a blameless life. I certainly haven't. But you have to be comfortable with what you've done, since everybody's going to know about it."

"I don't know if I could live in that kind of goldfish bowl."

"You'd get used to the pleasure of watching the other fish. There's always that." She stood up. "Be good to her," she said softly.

He watched her go back to the kitchen, her walk brisk and economical, and her parting words, which he felt carried the moral authority of Ellen's dead father, reverberating through his mind.

• • •

He reached the cabin at the ranch shortly before one o'clock, feeling increasingly guilty about having deserted Sam the night before. Gordon was enough of a man to know when he hadn't a leg to stand on, and his conscience was pricked further when he saw on his bed a piece of paper, folded over once. He picked it up and read it:

Gordon: You rat. You invite me up to go fishing with you, then leave me to myself most of the time. Last night was the final straw! I waited for you at the Bamboo Garden until nine fifteen, and finally had to order dinner because they were closing. If you care (which I doubt) and if you want to do anything about it (which I doubt even more), I'll be working the East Buchanan this afternoon. Having wonderful fishing trip; wish you were here. Sam.

Gordon smiled. The scolding was deserved, but he knew his friend well enough to realize that putting it on paper had gotten the spleen out of Sam's system. He began crumpling the paper, then stopped, deciding to save it as a tonic that could be applied whenever he might be feeling too pleased with himself. He also realized now that his unmannerly behavior had been the proximate cause of Sam's arriving at the ranch later than he otherwise would have, and hence, by sheer chance, preventing Ellen's house from burning down. He paced restlessly around the cabin for a moment. This had been the third attempt on her life, and it was considerably more bold and overt than the previous two. In view of the direction his relations with her had taken, he was unwilling to leave matters to chance or wait for the federal agents to move against Radio and his men. That could take days and leave Radio with an opportunity to strike again. A course of action had been forming in Gordon's mind all day long, and this settled it.

But first there were amends to be made to Sam, so Gordon set out for the East Buchanan. The river runs generally parallel to the state highway, sometimes just below it and sometimes as much as two hundred feet below, depending on the terrain. He found Sam's car parked in a turnout where the road had begun to climb above the water. A heavily rutted dirt path led down to the river 60 feet below, where he could see Sam flogging the water. After putting on his waders and vest, Gordon picked up his favorite fly rod, took two cold beers from the cooler, and started down to see his friend.

By now it was warm in the shade and hot in the direct sunlight. He reached the river and walked downstream to where Sam was fishing a riffle, his back to Gordon and the road.

"Any luck?"

Sam turned around. "Nice to see you for a change," he said sarcastically. "So glad you could make it."

"I asked how the fishing was."

"Not bad. I've caught a couple."

"How big?"

"Ten, eleven inches."

"That calls for a celebration." Gordon held up the beers. "Care to join me?"

Sam paused long enough to satisfy himself that he had appeared uninterested. "Why not," he said.

He waded ashore and joined Gordon in the shade of a pine tree. Each man took a couple of swallows of beer before Gordon finally spoke.

"Look, Sam, I don't suppose it'll do any good to say I'm sorry. I didn't mean to leave you hanging here, but things just kept happening and finally there was no way I could get hold of you."

Sam took another pull at the beer bottle. "I see," he said.

"I apologize. I really do."

"Don't start blubbering, man. The apology's accepted."

"Thanks. It's good to have you on my side again, because I'm going to be needing your help."

"I'll do what I can, but I've never been a best man before."

"That's not what I meant — at least not yet. No, I want you to come with me tonight to Radio's camp after dark and help me find the rifle that killed Dan McHenry."

Sam, who was taking a sip of his beer, gagged and aspirated. He stood clutching his chest and coughing violently from its depths. Gordon pressed on.

"It's the only way to get to the bottom of this. Baca's said himself that the gun is the missing piece in the picture. If the rifle that's missing from the McHenry house is with at Radio's camp, it'll prove that Ellen didn't kill her brother and that one of them did. There's close to a full moon tonight, so we can park a mile or so from the camp and kind of sneak up on it. When they turn in, we can look around to at least see where it might be. It's a long shot, I know, but it's the best chance I see right now."

Sam, who had finally stopped wheezing,. stared at Gordon with his mouth open slightly, then looked at the label on the beer bottle.

"This stuff must be affecting my thought processes," he said. "Let me tell you what I thought I just heard. It sounded to me as if you were suggesting that you and I go up to a group campsite inhabited by heavily armed psychos in the middle of the night and risk our health, if not our lives, poking around looking for something that may not even be there. Surely that's not what you said."

"Sam. I thought I could count on you."

"Up to a point. But when you get beyond reason, deal me out. That's crazy and dangerous, Gordon, and I'm not going to do it. Period, finito, end of discussion."

"Then I'll go alone."

"Don't be melodramatic."

"I will."

Sam stood up and finished his beer. "You know something. It's been over 48 hours since you and I have been fishing together. That's what we came here for, isn't it? Let's get some fishing done and pick up this discussion again at the end of the day."

"Fair enough," Gordon said after a pause. "Are we keeping count to decide who buys dinner?

"I suppose." Sam sighed. "Though I don't know why. You always win."

"I'll spot you the two fish you've already caught."

"You're on."

"What are you using?"

"Pheasant Tail nymph."

Gordon shook his head. "That'll catch you some fish, but in this fast water, with no weed beds to speak of, a large Golden Stone Nymph would be better."

"So show me."

• • •

It was a fine, warm afternoon, and both men thoroughly enjoyed their time on the water. Each whooped with delight when he caught a fish, and the other applauded as it was brought in and released. At three o'clock, a caddis hatch began, and they fished dry flies for an hour. They broke for the day at five. Gordon had caught ten fish to Sam's six (two of them while Sam was drying off from having fallen into the river after stepping on a mossy rock) so even with the head start, Sam was on the hook for dinner.

Gordon called Ellen and was pleasantly surprised when she agreed to join him and Sam for dinner at the Stage Stop. The three of them settled in at the same back booth Gordon and Baca had shared two nights earlier. Once dinner was ordered, Gordon laid out his plan for a visit to Radio's camp. When he finished, there was a moment of silence.

"Isn't that the craziest thing you ever heard in your life?" asked Sam.

"I'm coming along," said Ellen. Both men protested, but she waved them off. "My stake in this is bigger than either of yours, and I know the territory better. Besides, I'm willing to try anything to dispel this cloud hanging over me. Deal me in."

"I don't know," Sam said.

"It's very gallant of you to do this," she said, then, looking at Sam, "and particularly you, since you came up here to go fishing and your friend sort of dragged you into it. But if the rifle that killed my brother is at that camp, I'd be letting down everything my family ever stood for if I didn't move heaven and earth to find it. So I'm coming with the two of you, and that's that."

"The two of us," Sam moaned.

They continued discussing their plans for the evening over dinner in the hushed voices of conspirators, and by the end of the meal Sam was getting into the spirit of the occasion. When he reached for the check, Gordon grabbed it instead.

"It's the least I can do," he said with a smile. "This could be your final meal."

• • •

"You were going to go without a gun?" Ellen asked. "That's crazy. If they're armed we need to protect ourselves."

"Don't look at me," Gordon said. "I'd hardly know which end to point and it would be pure luck if I hit anything I was shooting at."

"Same here," said Sam.

They were in the front room of the main house at the ranch. It was nine o'clock, time to leave. Ellen shook her head and moved over to the gun case. Taking a key from her pocket, she opened the sliding glass door and removed a rifle. After inspecting it to make sure it wasn't loaded, she cocked it to test the action, which met with her approval.

"I guess it's up to me," she said. From the cupboard at the foot of the gun case she removed a box of cartridges. "Let's go."

Gordon drove them in the Cherokee, with Ellen in the front and Sam in the back. It took forty five minutes to reach a turnout on the road about three quarters of a mile below where Radio and his followers were camped. The road went up a slight rise from where they parked, before descending into Sullivan Meadow, keeping them out of sight of the camp.

They got out of the car and closed the doors as softly as possible. Ellen took a loaded magazine from her jacket pocket and put it into the rifle.

"All right, what's the plan?" she asked.

"I don't know if you can call it a plan," Gordon said. "I thought we'd try to get close enough to the camp to see what they're doing. If it looks like we can get closer once everybody's asleep, we'll do it, and look around as much as we can."

"And I assume," said Sam, "that if upon further inspection, this escapade looks as foolhardy as when it was first proposed, we'll quietly retreat to the car and return to safety."

"So I guess the idea is that my rifle and I stay back in the trees to provide cover, just in case," Ellen said.

Gordon nodded. "I don't think it'll be necessary, but yes."

"Do you have an extra key for the Cherokee?"

"Good point." He reached under the rim of the front tire and plucked the spare he kept on a magnet there.

"Do you keep that there in the city?" asked Sam.

"Only on fishing trips. I locked the keys in it one day last year and had to walk three miles in my waders to the nearest phone to call for help. Never again."

"Our fearless leader," said Sam.

"I just thought of something," interjected Ellen. "Maybe you should turn the car around so it's pointing back home. Just in case we have to leave in a hurry."

"I don't think we'll need to, but let's do it. Just to be safe."

"Now that you mention it," Sam said, "maybe someone should stay behind with the car in case we need to get it going in a hurry. I'll volunteer."

Gordon and Ellen ignored the last remark. When the Cherokee was turned around, they all started up the road toward the meadow. The moon, only a day or two away from being full, provided enough light for them to see their way, though at some points it fell behind the tops of the pines and threw the road into dark shadow.

"Step carefully," Ellen said. "The rattlesnakes come out at night."

"Terrific," said Sam.

After a few minutes, they topped the rise and looked down a gentle slope toward the meadow. The cluster of tents, horses, and vehicles looked much as Gordon remembered it from the previous week. Two campfires were burning, and about a dozen men were sitting or standing near them, or just milling around. Several lanterns on ropes or tables illuminated the main camp area.

"We can get closer if we follow the trees by the creek," Gordon whispered.

"Go ahead," said Ellen. "I'm going to get behind that tree," she pointed to a solitary pine at their right. "It'll give me a good overview of their camp and a fast track back to the car."

"What's our fast track back to the car?" asked Sam.

"Don't worry about it," Gordon said. He turned to Ellen and kissed her gently. "Back in a bit."

Gordon and Sam crept down the hill to the creek, then followed it upstream to the meadow. By wading across at a shallow spot and taking cover in the trees on the side opposite the camp, they were able to get within 75 yards of it. There they sat for a few minutes, able to make out an occasional word or phrase being spoken by the campfires.

After a while, Radio emerged from the largest tent, which had a lantern on inside. All the men straightened up as he approached.

"It's ten thirty, gentlemen," he said. "Time to bunk down." He put his hand over his heart, and the others did the same. "Jerry."

The man he addressed leaned down and put a cassette into a boom box by one of the campfires. After half a minute, an orchestral rendition of "The Star Spangled Banner" began to play, the music resonating through the thin mountain air. It sounded like the tinny renditions that radio stations used to play to sign on and off for the day. All the men were standing motionless, as if in rapture.

When the music ended, Radio lowered his hand to his side. "Thank you, Jerry. Again at six thirty tomorrow morning. I trust there's no reason for the sheriff to interrupt our sleep tonight." There were a few chuckles. Radio looked up at the stars, took a deep breath, and walked slowly to the large tent. The other men moved into their various tents and Jerry went to the creek with a bucket. He came back twice to douse the two fires, then slipped into one of the tents. Five minutes after the end of the music, the camp was dark and silent.

"Well," said Sam, "are you ready to go back now?"

"Let's give them half an hour to fall asleep, then make our move."

The half hour lasted a long time. Even though the day had been warm, it was late in the season and the night was growing steadily colder. When they had been moving, Gordon and Sam didn't notice the temperature, but sitting in one place they did. The stillness of the night was interrupted only occasionally by a light breeze and the sound of an occasional owl hooting or cow bell clanging.

At five minutes past eleven, Gordon nudged Sam and they got up. They walked along the edge of the stream and quietly waded across at a shallow spot, then moved into the meadow, crouched down in the grass about fifty yards from the camp and surveyed it. Gordon realized, more than he had a week ago, that it was laid out like a compound. The center area where the campfires had been burning was flanked by parallel rows of three tents. The large tent, Radio's, took up one end and the other was open. The pickups and sport utility vehicles were parked around the perimeter or between the tents.

"Now what?" whispered Sam.

"We go very quietly through there, looking for any rifle we can find. The one we're looking for has the initials D.M. carved into the butt with an amateur hand. I have a pocket flashlight we can use to check a gun butt up close, but otherwise we use the light of the moon only."

"All right, but let's at least start with the perimeter and only go in if we have to." Gordon nodded.

Moving slowly and cautiously, they circled the camp and wound up behind Radio's tent, where two vehicles were parked. One was an Explorer that had three rifles in its back. Gordon flashed the light inside it quickly, then shut it off. No good. He couldn't make out enough detail in the short time he dared leave the light on. With the adjacent pickup truck, however, he was able to walk up behind the cab and quickly flash the light over the butts of the rifles on its rack. None of them had the initials he was looking for, but he at least could tell that for a certainty. He held very still after he switched the light off, but the camp remained absolutely silent and motionless. They worked their way around the perimeter, with Sam covering Gordon's rear flank as he approached the parked vehicles.

In a tense quarter-hour, they examined everything they could get to from outside the compound of tents. That left two pickups and two sport utility vehicles parked between the tents so that their rears were facing into the camping area. Both pickups had gun racks that held rifles.

"We have to check those out," Gordon whispered. "This is where I really need you. When I go up to one of the trucks, just keep scanning the camp. If you see anything move at all, pat me on the butt and we'll get behind whatever we can and hope they don't see us."

"I don't think we should go in there."

"Shut up. You're making too much noise."

With a careful, measured tread, they entered the camping area. Gordon approached the first pickup, his body coiled with tension. As he stepped gently between the tent and the vehicle, he realized he was close enough to the former to hear the deep, steady breathing of the sleeping men inside. When he turned the light on, the gentle rasp of the switch sounded like a firecracker to him, but the breathing inside the tent continued its regular pattern. The missing rifle wasn't there.

The instant he switched the flashlight off, Sam touched him on the seat.

He turned and dropped to his knees. As his head dropped behind the tent, he could see the flap of the last tent on the opposite side being opened and a man beginning to emerge. Gordon sat without breathing for what seemed forever, until he heard the faint sound of a steady stream of urine hitting the grass of the meadow. He and Sam exhaled simultaneously. A moment later they heard the rustle of the tent flap being pulled back into place.

They waited for a moment, then Sam turned to Gordon and silently mouthed the words, "Let's get out of here." Gordon shook his head and pointed to the other pickup across the camp area from them. With extreme care, they made their way to it. It was parked so there was barely a foot of space between it and the tents on either side. Three rifles hung in the gun rack, two with their butts on the driver's side and the one in the middle with its butt on the passenger side. Gordon held the side of the pickup tightly to avoid brushing the tent as he moved along sideways. The two rifles on the driver's side weren't what he was looking for. He carefully worked his way back outside the tight space and squeezed gingerly along the other side of the pickup. He reached the back of the cab and flicked his pocket light quickly on and off again.

There it was.

He held his breath for a minute, unable to believe what he had just seen. Then he turned the light on again and left it on for a full five seconds. The initials D.M. were carved on the butt, amateurishly with a pocket knife of some sort. Without doubt, this was the deer rifle that was missing from the McHenry residence, the gun that could prove Ellen McHenry hadn't killed her brother.

Gordon turned to Sam and gave the thumbs-up sign with his left hand, then gestured to the open end of the camp to signal that it was time to go. He eased out of the narrow opening between the pickup and the tent, and Sam took three steps backward to let him out.

If Sam had taken only two steps backward, the mission would have been a triumphant success. But halfway through the third step, his left heel met one of the rocks that formed the campfire circle, and he lost his balance. Twisting and throwing out a hand to break his fall, he pushed over a folding chair on which the pots and pans used to cook that evening's meal had been drying. They hit the ground with a spectacular clatter that could probably have been heard half way to Harperville.

Before Gordon even had a chance to think, men were pouring out of tents and lights were being shined in his eyes. Instinctively, he made a break for the edge of the camping area, but after he had run only a few steps, he was roughly tackled by two men, who brought him to earth hard enough to put a deep gash on his chin. From the derisive remarks being made a few feet away, he could tell that Sam had been caught as well.

The two men picked Gordon up and led him back to the center of the camping area, where Sam was also being detained. By now, several lanterns had been lit and the area was well illuminated. Hart Lee Bowen emerged from the group of the men and stood before Gordon. A nasty smile formed on his face.

"Well look what we have here. Hey, boss!"

Radio moved into sight. "Mr. Gordon," he said. "What an unexpected pleasure. But I could have saved you a trip up here. The fishing isn't any better at night than during the day."

The camp followers laughed boisterously. Gordon said nothing, and after a moment Radio continued.

"On the other hand, you probably wouldn't have listened. You see, gentlemen," he addressed the others, "Mr. Gordon has a little problem with the king's English. I've told him on several occasions that we'd rather he didn't come visit us up here, so what does he do? He comes up after hours when he thinks we're asleep and won't notice." He paused. "I'm afraid that's a bit rude, and I think we need to indicate our displeasure. Hart Lee, since Mr. Gordon doesn't seem to be too good with words, maybe we should make our displeasure known through some non-verbal communication. Do you think you could do that?"

"Sure thing." Bowen put his flashlight in a hip pocket and moved directly in front of Gordon and about two feet away. Leering all the while, he rocked slightly on the balls of his feet for a few seconds, then leaned forward and spat in Gordon's face. Before that even registered, Bowen threw a vicious punch with his right hand, landing it in the abdomen, just below the ribs. The air went out of Gordon at once, and his knees buckled, leaving him held up by the men on either side of him."

"Excellent, Hart Lee. Well done."

"Thanks, boss."

"Do you understand me now, Mr. Gordon?"

Gordon tried to speak but couldn't. He was gasping for breath, like a fish out of water.

"Silence generally implies consent, so I'll assume we've made ourselves clear. Now the next question is what do we do with you? The way I see it, you were trespassing. And that reminds me of the story about the rancher who caught three men trespassing on his property. Do you know what he told them?"

Gordon and Sam said nothing.

"He said, 'Gentlemen, there are three of you, and I only have two bullets. Which one of you wants to be hanged?'" He guffawed loudly, and the other men laughed as well. Gordon had recovered enough from Bowen's blow to be conscious, for the first time, of the raw fear he felt.

"I have an idea," said Sam. "I think you've made your point very well, and by the way, I'm glad you made it on my friend and not me, but seeing as how we understand each other now, how about letting us go if we promise not to come back and bother you again."

The men laughed again.

"Does that mean no?" Sam asked.

"You've been getting in my face for a week now," Radio said to Gordon, "and I mean to put an end to it. One way or another, you and your friend are going to be treated like the enemies of freedom you are."

"Hey, boss," said Bowen. "How about if we tie them to that tree overnight," he gestured to a pine standing by itself about fifty feet from the camp, "and use them for target practice tomorrow morning."

A murmur rippled through the group, but Radio shook his head. "Let's settle it now. You gave me an idea with the tree, though, Hart Lee." He turned to another of the men. "Jason, you were showing us a couple of weeks ago how to make a noose. Can you do it now?"

"Sure thing."

"Then get to it. Two of them. Who has the handcuffs?"

"I do," said George Horton.

"Cuff their hands behind their backs. You two, get a pair of horses for our guests of honor. Let's take a few minutes to get dressed for the occasion, then reassemble at the tree with the ropes, horses and prisoners."

Gordon and Sam were allowed to sit down by one of the tents, but two armed men kept watch over them from a distance of a few feet, so any thought of escape, or even conversation, was impossible. Gordon tried to fight down the fear he felt by concentrating on the situation. Surely, Ellen must be going for help now; At least there was that. If only he could stall long enough for it to arrive. But how? And in the event he couldn't, there was something he needed to say.

"Sam, I'm sorry."

"Again? I told you this was crazy. Anyway, he can't be serious about hanging us. He'd have to be a psychopath."

At that point, Jason walked past them with two lengths of rope, one of which had already been fitted into a noose.

"You were saying? asked Gordon."

They sat in silence for another minute, then Horton walked over to them, waving the guards back a few feet.

"I'm sorry about this, Mr. Gordon," he said softly. "I'd say something if I thought it would do any good, but I'm afraid your goose is cooked."

Sam's eyes began to widen. Gordon hesitated a moment, then replied, "I appreciate the thought, anyway." Horton cocked his head slightly to the side as Gordon continued, "Can I ask you one question, George?"

"You can always ask."

"Who owns the Dodge pickup across the way there?" He nodded toward the vehicle that carried Dan McHenry's rifle.

"I do," Horton said. "Why do you ask?"

"I was thinking of buying one." Gordon smiled. "Guess I waited too long."

"It *is* a nice truck," Horton said. "Well, so long. Or maybe I should say good bye." He shook his head. "You shouldn't have got involved."

Gordon thought, as Horton walked away, that without knowing it, he had been a bigger help to the two prisoners than he ever intended to be.

• • •

Several minutes later, Radio and the other men came by for the prisoners. Gordon and Sam were led, with no undue gentleness, to a lone pine tree thirty yards outside the camp's perimeter. A rope with a noose at its end had been thrown over a branch on each side of the tree, ten to twelve feet up. One of the pickup trucks that had been parked outside the camp area had been moved so it was now parked a few feet from the tree, facing away. Bowen put one of the nooses around Gordon's neck, while another man did the same to Sam.

"I'm afraid this rope's a bit scratchy," he said insinuatingly, "but then that's probably going to be the least of your problems."

"I've never liked wearing a necktie," Gordon replied.

"A comedian, huh?" grunted Bowen.

Two horses were led up to the tree and put in position under the branches, then the prisoners were helped into the saddle. The nooses were pulled tightly enough around their necks that they had to sit unnaturally high to keep from choking slightly. The other ends of the ropes were fastened to the sides of the pickup truck. Gordon hadn't believed Radio at first, but there was little doubting the seriousness of the situation now. With the horses out from under them, Gordon and Sam would be left dangling a foot and a half off the ground as they slowly choked to death. Only a few words stood between a horrible end for him and Sam, and Gordon hoped he had chosen those words well.

Radio stepped up in front of them.

"Gentlemen," he said, "Summit County just won't be the same without you. You've been a great nuisance to me, but I'm sorry it had to end like this. Do you have any last words?"

"I hope they do this to you," Sam said.

"Right you are, my friend, and we'll be meeting in hell later on. But the law can't catch me and the devil doesn't want me. How about you, Gordon?"

"You're making a mistake, Radio."

"I said last words. Sermons don't count. All right, gentlemen. On the count of three, let's tell these horses to giddy-up back where they came from and let our guests enjoy some neck-stretching exercise. One."

"You've got it all wrong, Radio." Gordon shouted. He was desperately trying to keep the fear out of his voice. "Ellen McHenry didn't kill her brother. The motive for that killing wasn't greed or defense of family. It was love."

"Two."

"Radio! The gun that killed Dan McHenry is in this camp."

Radio had just begun the downward motion of his hand to accompany the third count, but froze the gesture instantly. For thirty seconds that seemed to last forever, he looked hard at Gordon, making a mental calculation.

"On second thought, perhaps we shouldn't be so hasty," Radio said. "Our visitors may still be worth something to us alive. Untie those ropes and get the handcuffs off for a minute." This was done, and Gordon and Sam quickly removed the ropes around their necks. "Why don't you get down off your high horse and let's talk."

They dismounted, and Gordon looked around. They were surrounded, but at least not bound. He felt certain that if he could stall for another hour, maybe an hour and a half at the outside, help would arrive.

"All right," Radio said. "Where's the gun."

"Not so fast. I have information that's going to be very valuable to you, and I want to set some terms for letting you have it."

"If it comes right down to it, we can make you tell."

"Maybe, but it would take time and cause legal problems. You'd be better off dealing than trying any rough stuff."

Radio stroked his chin for a few seconds. "I need a few minutes to think about this," he said. "Jerry, Hart Lee! Take these gentlemen back to my tent. There's a folding table in it, where the legs are joined at the bottom. Handcuff them, one hand each, around a table leg so they can't go anywhere without taking the table with them. Then keep watch on them until I get there. Got that?"

Bowen smiled. "Can I put Mortimer in with them?" he asked.

"Mortimer?" said Sam.

"His pet rattlesnake," said Radio. "Not right now, Hart Lee, but we'll keep the option open for phase two of the negotiations. Go on. And if they look like they're even thinking of escaping, shoot to kill."

Bowen smiled wickedly. "I like shooting to kill," he said.

They started back to the camp, four abreast. Bowen was to Gordon's left, holding an arm with his right hand and a revolver in his left hand. Sam was to Gordon's right, being held by Jerry's left hand, while Jerry carried a lantern in his right hand. Gordon was pleased. Time was going by, and time was his ally. With each passing minute, Ellen was getting closer to help and help was getting closer to them.

"You ever been bitten by a rattlesnake?" Bowen asked conversationally.

"Not that I can remember," Gordon replied.

"You'd remember," Bowen continued. "The pain is like nothing you've ever experienced. It feels like someone's standing inside your blood vessels with a flamethrower. Your leg or arm or wherever you got bit swells up something nasty, and even if you're lucky enough to live, there can be a permanent loss of feeling. Yes sir, I surely would like to introduce you to Mortimer tonight."

A shot rang out, and the lantern in Jerry's hand shattered, throwing them into the fading moonlight illuminating the meadow.

Gordon reacted instantaneously. Bowen had instinctively let go of him and looked to see where the shot came from. Gordon threw his left elbow upward as hard as he could and caught Bowen directly under the chin. His head snapped backward, and he crumpled to the ground unconscious. Gordon took the revolver from his hand.

Another shot was fired, and this time it sounded as if the bullet hit metal. A second later, the pickup to which Gordon and Sam had been tied burst into a ball of flame. Sam and Jerry were grappling with each other. Men were running in all directions, looking for cover. Gordon moved behind Jerry, grabbed a shoulder for ballast, then brought the butt of Bowen's gun down hard on the back of his head. He dropped like a lead weight.

"This way," Gordon said.

The third and fourth shots came as he and Sam raced across the meadow. Chaos reigned, and for an instant the prisoners had been forgotten. They jumped across the creek in two bounds, reached the shelter of the woods and looked back. No one was following them.

"The lady can shoot, can't she?" Gordon said.

"She might have hit me," Sam gasped.

"No time to worry about that. We need to get out of here." They began working back toward the road along the edge of the forest, the way they had originally come. It seemed to be taking five times as long to get out as it had to come in. There were no more gunshots, and after a few moments of calm, just as Gordon and Sam reached the point where the forest met the road, three men with flashlights began to move toward the trees where they had been a few moments earlier. By the light of the flaming truck, which was gradually burning down, the two fugitives could see that Bowen was just beginning to sit up groggily. Gordon finally exhaled, but no sooner had he done that than he heard a sound that made him shiver with fear.

An engine started in the meadow below them, and the lights of one of the pickups came on.

Gordon turned to Sam. "They're coming after us. I hope you can run a quarter of a mile in a minute," he said, "because your life might depend on it."

They raced down the road as fast as they could. The moon had moved lower and was more behind the trees, so the visibility was worse than it had been on the way in. At any second, they expected to be caught in the glare of the pickup's headlights, which would be fatal. Gordon tried to visualize himself sprinting toward the basket on a fast break.

His foot hit something, maybe a rut in the road, and his ankle turned. Shouting involuntarily from the pain, he flew through the air head first, letting go of the gun, which clattered into the darkness. He landed hard on the earth and gravel, scraping the palms of his hands and the front of his body as he skidded forward. Sam stopped.

"Keep going!" Gordon screamed. He got to his feet, ankle throbbing, and looked for the gun, but couldn't see it. He began to run again, willing himself to do it through the pain. Even with the injury, he was able to keep pace with Sam, who was about a hundred feet ahead.

Ellen was standing by the Cherokee, rifle in hand. The moment it was in sight, Gordon shouted, "They're coming after us." At the same instant, the headlights of the pickup came into sight over the rise behind him. Ellen set her rifle in the back seat, leaped behind the wheel, and started the engine as Sam arrived and dived into the passenger's seat in front. Gordon pulled up seconds later and climbed into the back. Ellen stepped on the accelerator as he was closing the door, and the car shot forward.

The pickup was less than a hundred yards behind them when they pulled on to the road and closed to 75 yards before they were able to match its speed. Ellen drove without fear. They were going 45 to 50 miles an hour on a narrow, winding dirt road that was never meant to be driven faster than 25. The bouncing and jostling from the rough surface of the road would have made Gordon nauseous if not for the fact that he was too frightened to be sick.

"Are we gaining?" asked Ellen.

"No, but we're not losing."

"Are you all right?"

"No, but just keep driving."

The road was running through deep forest, and the surrounding trees shut out the moon, leaving them in almost total darkness. Even with the bright headlights on, it was hard to see much ahead. Gordon was impressed with Ellen's fearlessness and thought some of it might have to do with knowing the road well. Even so, as he looked back and saw the lights of the pursuing pickup, he realized it might not be enough. Once they reached the state highway, with its longer stretches of straight, well-paved road, the pickup, with its more powerful engine, would probably overtake them.

"Is there any place we can get off this road and hide?" he asked.

"Not that I know of," she said. "Why?"

"Never mind." Then, almost as an afterthought, "We found the rifle."

"Where?"

"George Horton has it on a rack in his pickup truck."

"George?"

"Don't slow down!"

"Sorry."

They screeched around a curve and came to a long, straight piece of road that ran for about two hundred yards, with forest on their left and an open patch of meadow on the right. As Ellen gunned the car forward, Gordon looked behind. Was it his imagination, or was the pickup a little closer than it had been?

"Oh my God!" cried Ellen, as a large doe bounded out of the woods in front of the Cherokee. It was past them in an instant, but its rear hooves could not have missed the front headlight by more than inches. She slammed on the brakes by instinct, and the pickup drew closer.

"Don't stop!" screamed Gordon.

"I hope her boyfriend's coming behind her," said Sam.

He was, and he landed on the road a second later, directly in front of the pursuing pickup. Its driver flinched left, but the vehicle struck the large buck a fatal blow in the midsection, then skidded to the left and crashed into a pine tree. The last thing Gordon noticed as Ellen turned the corner that ended the straightaway, was that both its lights were out, making pursuit hopeless even if the truck could still run.

"You can slow down now," he said.

"What happened?" asked Sam.

"Just what you hoped for. They hit a deer and skidded into a tree."

"People can get killed that way," Ellen said.

"It was a pretty big truck, so they may be all right," Gordon said, "but I don't think they're driving any farther tonight."

They reached the bottom of the dirt road, turned right, crossed the cattle guard, and drove in silence for several minutes.

"This has been a night," Sam finally said.

"It's only the beginning," Gordon said.

Friday September 17

It was two thirty in the morning, and Gordon, Ellen and Sam were sitting before the fire in the living room of the main house at the ranch. It had taken them very little time to decide to call Baca at home, never mind the hour. When he heard that Gordon had found Dan McHenry's gun at Radio's encampment, the sheriff said he'd be over promptly. Gordon, aching all over, was partially reclined on the couch, with Ellen snuggled against him and a scotch and soda in hand. Sam was pacing nervously in front of the fire.

"I can't believe you found the rifle," Ellen said. "This is the first good news I've had in six months."

"And I can't believe your shooting and driving," said Gordon. "It took real presence of mind to wait until you did to shoot out that lantern."

"What I can't believe," said Sam, "is that we were crazy enough to go up there in the first place. I'm sorry, but Rex Radio is not playing with a full deck, and he hasn't exactly surrounded himself with nice people. Mortimer, indeed."

"I couldn't hear what was being said down there," Ellen said, "but it gave me the willies when they played the national anthem before going to bed. It just — it was wrong, somehow."

"It was creepy," said Gordon, "no doubt about it. But so's everything having to do with them. The weapons, the snakes, the paranoia." He leaned over and gave her a peck on the cheek. "The worst is over now."

Baca drove up shortly before three o'clock and walked through the door, unshaven but in uniform, with a black case in his hand. Ellen made a pot of coffee, and Gordon described the evening's events in complete detail as Baca listened intently, saying nothing until the story was over. Then he spoke.

"You know, don't you, that what you did was unbelievably foolhardy. By all rights, you and your friend should be dead right now. Think about it. And you," he turned to Ellen, "are lucky you didn't start a forest fire by shooting at that pickup."

He opened the black case and took out a laptop computer. "However," he said, "I guess God watches over fools. And we now have what may be the first break in the murder of Dan McHenry. At any rate, if you can give me a statement, I have something to take to the judge and get a search warrant." He tapped and clicked on the computer. "Budget, schedule, here we are — warrant." He looked up. "I have a standard form for all these things."

"Just out of curiosity," Gordon said, "how much money do the taxpayers of Summit County spend on your computer systems?"

"Whatever I ask them to," Baca said. "Now let's get on with it. All right, I the undersigned do solemnly affirm, etcetera, etcetera, that at approximately eleven o'clock on the night of September 16th — no, take out the time; the night of September 16th — I visited an encampment at the area commonly known as Sullivan Meadows on the West Fork of the Buchanan River."

"That's one way of putting it," Gordon said.

"In this case, it's best to leave out the details. Trust me." He began typing again, "Among the persons present who were known to me were Rex Radio, Hart Lee Bowen, and George Horton."

"Don't you want me to give a statement?"

"No. It's faster this way. Did your friend see the gun?"

"Just me."

"Fine. In the course of the visit, I was able to see several high-caliber rifles of the type used for hunting ..."

"Numerous would be a more descriptive word than several."

Baca changed the word and continued, "Openly displayed on racks in vehicles parked in the vicinity of the campsite. At one point in the visit, I chanced to be near one of those vehicles ..."

"Chanced? I risked my neck to get up close to it."

Baca glared at him. "Do you want me to get this search warrant or not? If I tell the judge you went up there after dark and sneaked around the campsite with a flashlight and a confederate, he might start asking some embarrassing questions and bring the proceedings to a halt. Like I said, let's keep it basic."

"Write what you want. I'll sign anything."

"That's more like it. All right, and was able to get a close look at the three guns in its rack. One of those guns was a rifle that had the initials D.M. carved into its butt in what appeared to be a childish hand. Because of previous conversations with Ellen McHenry, I knew that a gun matching that description had disappeared from her house and was being sought as evidence in the death of her brother, Daniel. Recognizing the importance of my discovery, I left the encampment as hastily as possible ..."

Gordon, Sam, and Ellen broke into laughter. "You could say that again," Gordon said.

"And promptly notified the authorities of the existence of this weapon at this location. Et cetera, et cetera, et cetera. That sound okay?"

"Fine."

Baca put a floppy disk in the laptop, copied the document to it, and handed it to Ellen. "Can you run that off for me?" he asked.

She nodded and went off.

"So what happens now?" Sam asked.

Baca looked at his watch. "It's a little after three thirty right now. The judge gets up at five thirty, so I'll call him then. He can probably get to the courthouse by six thirty. Figure half an hour to an hour for me to make my case and get the warrant signed. After that, we serve it."

"You're not going up there by yourself?" asked Gordon.

The sheriff gave him a hard stare. "I'm trying to figure out what I've done that's dumb enough to make you ask a question like that. Of course I'm not going up there alone, you idiot!" he bellowed. "There are twelve sheriff's deputies in Summit County, and every last man jack of them is going to be with me. And a couple of Highway Patrol units, too. And before I even go to the judge, I'm calling Boyd at ATF and telling him to be on stand-by. It may not be necessary, but I don't want anybody — anybody! — to be able to say that I served a warrant on Rex Radio and underestimated him."

They greeted his outburst with silence, which Gordon finally broke.

"I want to come, too," he said, quietly.

Baca paused and stroked his chin. His fingers rasped over the stubble.

"According to Hoyle, I should say no. On the other hand, you found the gun we've been looking for and the cache of weapons in that mine, so I probably owe you the right to see this through. All right, you can come. But on two conditions. You have to stay out of sight when we get there, and you have to do whatever I tell you. I can't have you getting underfoot."

"Fair enough," Gordon replied. "Are you up for it, Sam?"

"I'm in too far to quit now," Sam said.

Ellen came back with the printout of the affidavit, and Gordon signed it after only a cursory reading. Baca put it in his case and prepared to leave.

"By the time we get the paperwork done and all the men together, it'll probably be eight o'clock," he said. "Meet us in front of the courthouse then."

"We'll be there," said Gordon. "And if for some reason you're ready early, we'll be at Kitty's having breakfast."

They shook hands, looking each other in the eye.

"This is going to come to a head today," said Baca, "and I have a feeling it isn't going to be what we expect."

• • •

After Baca left, Gordon and Sam took long, hot showers. Gordon ached all over. His leg muscles were stiff from squatting and running; the cut in his chin was in need of a stitch or two; the palms of his hands were scraped raw from the fall and hurt whenever he touched anything; there was a nasty welt on his stomach where Bowen had hit him; his torso, thighs, knees and shins were scraped and bruised from being tackled at the campground and the fall he took while he and Sam were fleeing; and his right ankle was swollen, throbbing, and could barely support his weight. Yet he was a happy man. He had found the missing gun and directed suspicion away from the woman he regarded with ever-increasing affection. It was the first time in his life that he had put himself out to a considerable extent for anyone else, and he enjoyed the feeling that accompanied it. After washing and dressing, he accepted another drink from Ellen, then fell asleep sitting up on her couch. He napped for an hour and a half until she awakened him at six o'clock. The ankle was worse after the rest, so he took a couple of Ibuprofen before he and Sam drove into town.

They arrived at Mom's Cafe shortly before seven. It was already three-quarters full and humming with conversation. Kitty saw them as they sat down and glided over.

"It's on the house today, boys," she said. "Ellen told me all about last night. That was wonderful of you."

As Kitty poured his coffee, Gordon reflected that the way in which women communicated was a mystery to him. When could Ellen have talked with Kitty? Probably while he was asleep. Calling someone on the phone to talk about last night would have been the farthest thing from his mind.

"What's going to happen next?" Kitty asked.

"I guess they're going to execute the search warrant," Gordon said. "Then they'll run tests on the gun to match it with the bullet that killed Dan McHenry. After that, several people will have to answer some hard questions."

"What if it doesn't match?"

"I don't think that's going to be an issue. But even so, a lot of suspicion will be off Ellen because the missing gun that pointed to her was found somewhere else."

Kitty heaved a sigh of relief. "I'm so glad."

"You're going to have to mail the test results to me," Sam said. "I have to leave tomorrow morning. I promised my family I'd be back Saturday night."

"You're not going, too, are you?" she asked Gordon.

He shook his head. "I can get another week off easily enough," he said. "And when I go back, I'm giving a month's notice. I've been working for Howell, Burns & Bledsoe for almost twelve years. It's time to do something different."

"But how will you live?"

He smiled. "I have a little money set aside. Don't worry about that."

"Anyway," she said, "I'm glad you'll be staying a little longer."

"Not as glad as I am."

She was back in fifteen minutes with their breakfast. Gordon had never tried the blueberry pancakes before, but they were perfect. He and Sam were too tired to keep up much of a conversation, and part way into the meal, Gordon picked up a copy of the Summit County Echo. He remembered that he hadn't read the story of Dan McHenry's murder yesterday at lunch, so he set the front page beside his plate and started in. A banner headline proclaimed "Dan McHenry Murdered," and below it was an unfocused photograph of the meadow and a two-column drop head: "Rancher's Son Shot in Back While Fishing on Family Spread." The text read as follows:

> The murder of Daniel McHenry is still a mystery — at least, officially. Sheriff Mike Baca said yesterday that although his investigation has yielded a number of clues, he's not yet prepared to make an arrest.

Mr. McHenry, 33, was shot in the back Sunday morning, apparently while fishing at Twin Creek Ranch, where he was raised as a child. It was the first murder in Summit County since 1985, and certainly one of the most sensational crimes in the history of this area, going as far back as the shooting of Jacob Harper.

At the time of his death, Mr. McHenry was involved in another sensational event. A court trial on his challenge to the will of his father, cattleman Frank McHenry, was about two thirds completed.

The elder McHenry, it will be recalled, changed his will in March of this year, just days before his death of complications resulting from falling off his horse. Where previously he had left the ranch and the bulk of the estate to his son, who had been living an unconventional lifestyle in San Francisco, the will now being disputed in court leaves the ranch and nearly all other McHenry assets to Dan McHenry's sister, Ellen, his only sibling.

Owing to the prominence of the McHenry family and the esteem in which it is held locally for its long record of straight dealing and good works, the trial has generated immense local interest and controversy. It was recessed for a week on the Monday following Mr. McHenry's death. (A related story summarizing developments in the trial appears on page 7.)

Under California law, Daniel McHenry's estate could continue the challenge to the will, and the rumor mill has been humming with speculation that this could be the case. The Echo was unable to confirm this point, but it will undoubtedly be dealt with when the matter comes before the court Monday next.

The circumstances of Mr. McHenry's slaying were deceptively straightforward. According to Sheriff Baca, he had shown up at the ranch at approximately eight o'clock Sunday morning, having previously asked his sister for permission to go fishing on the old family homestead. Miss McHenry, to the surprise of many people, assented, saying she couldn't deny her brother access to the ranch that had so long been his home.

Mr. McHenry was fishing the meadow above the main house at the ranch, and apparently had that section of the property to himself. Miss McHenry and all the ranch hands told the sheriff they had left the ranch by shortly after nine o'clock. Only two out-of-town anglers who had been allowed to fish Aspen Creek remained on the ranch, and they were fishing the section downstream from the main ranch house and were entirely out of Mr. McHenry's sight, as was he from theirs. (There have been rumors that one of the fishermen caught and released a 19-inch Brown Trout, but again, those are unconfirmed.)

Shortly before ten o'clock those two fishermen heard a gunshot, which Baca believes was the one that killed Mr. McHenry. The sheriff said that evidence indicates the killer assumed a position in the trees on a dirt road that parallels the edge of the meadow, and is often used for transporting cattle.

The two fishermen who heard the shot (Sheriff Baca is refusing to divulge their names) moved up to the meadow area shortly after noon and found Mr. McHenry's body in the creek, where it had fallen in and come to rest against a shrub.

The sheriff refused to say what kind of weapon was used to commit the crime. "All I can tell you is that Dan McHenry was shot from behind at some distance with a rifle. You'll know more when we make an arrest," he said.

Pressed as to whether an arrest is imminent, Baca replied testily, "I can't answer that right now. It depends on whether we can put together certain key pieces of evidence."

And there the matter stands as we go to press Wednesday night.

The funeral for Mr. McHenry was held Wednesday morning at Saint Louis Catholic Church and was well attended. Father Malone's eulogy was widely remarked upon as having been outstanding, given the circumstances.

Mr. McHenry was born and reared in Summit County, but had been only a visitor to the area for the past dozen years. He lived in San Francisco, where he worked as a freelance writer and was active in conservative political causes.

In addition to his sister, he leaves a close friend, George Horton, of San Francisco.

Gordon set the paper down uneasily. He realized as he finished the story that something in it had brushed up against a corner of his mind, had reminded him of something he had seen or heard in the last week. He cleaned the last of the food off his plate and read the story again. This time, it hit him squarely between the eyes, and he sat up with a start.

He let his eyes wander around the room as he thought. Kitty was making the rounds with coffee, and the crowd had thinned out some, but there was still a buzz of conversation. He looked at the mounted deer head by the door. Every few seconds another remembered fact collided with his consciousness like a drumbeat, and they all backed up the first revelation. Gordon felt faintly sick. The truth, if that was what it was, meant that another life hung in the balance.

He leaned over the table and addressed Sam in a low voice. "I just thought of something that could be really big. We need to go fast."

Sam nodded, and the two of them slipped out of the cafe with a wave and a thank you to Kitty. They drove the three blocks to the courthouse, where Baca was overseeing eight deputies and four squad cars. Gordon took him aside.

"I just remembered something that could be really important, and I hope I'm wrong," he told the sheriff. "But we need to get to Radio's camp on the double."

Baca shook his head. "I don't have all my men yet."

"Tell the rest of them to follow us."

"Do you suppose you could tell me what this is all about?"

Gordon shook his head. "I can't. The only thing worse than being right would be telling you and being wrong. You'll have to trust me."

Baca stared silently into the distance.

"My hunches have been pretty good so far," Gordon said. "And if this one's right, it's a matter of life and death."

"Are you sure of that?"

"Not dead certain, but it looks like it. Let's say that given what I think is going on, you should take the men you've got and get up there as fast as you can, with lights flashing and sirens blaring."

Baca looked at Gordon for a full ten seconds, then turned to his assembled men. "Let's go," he snapped.

• • •

The drive up to Sullivan Meadows was only slightly less hair-raising than the drive down had been the night before. A convoy was formed with patrol cars in front of and behind Gordon's Cherokee. With the aid of sirens and flashing lights, they got to the dirt road as fast as it was possible for man and vehicle to do so. At that point, the lights and sirens went off, but they still drove up the road as fast as was marginally prudent. At the open meadow where the pursuers had foundered the previous night, the dead buck lay by the side of the road, its carcass beginning to bloat. The pickup had been abandoned where it crashed into a tree, its bed protruding slightly into the road. There was no sign of its occupants, so Gordon assumed they must have survived the collision without serious injury.

Despite their speed, they were too late. As soon as he drove over the rise leading to the meadow, Gordon could see that the tents, vehicles and men were gone. His eyes moved to the tree where he and Sam had been taken the night before, and a knot formed in his stomach. The burned-out hulk of the pickup Ellen had set afire the night before was still there, but next to it was another pickup. A rope led from the back of it over a tree branch and down to the neck of a man who was dangling lifelessly, his hands cuffed together behind him.

Baca, the deputies, Gordon and Sam drove to the spot and got out of their cars. Though the purple, contorted face delayed identification for a few seconds, it was clearly George Horton, hanged by a rope tied to his own pickup truck. They stood before him in a stunned silence that was broken when one of the deputies suddenly retched. He was followed by another, then by Sam. Gordon needed the full force of his will to hold down his own breakfast.

"Poor bastard," said Baca, turning to Gordon. "Was this what you were expecting?"

Gordon nodded. "Not a lynching, but I was afraid for George."

Baca put his arm around Gordon and walked him away from the grisly scene toward the spot where the camp had been. The grass of the meadow was still flattened where the tents had stood just hours before. Several pieces of litter, including two folding chairs and several cooking utensils, were strewn on the ground, suggesting a hasty departure.

"Do you want to talk about it?" the sheriff asked.

Gordon shook his head. "It's my fault," he said. "Dan McHenry's gun was on a rack in George's pickup — the same one the rope's tied to now. I practically shoved Radio's nose in it last night. When he connected George with the gun, it was probably all over."

"The gun's gone now."

"They probably took it with them. There were three guns in the rack, and they're all gone."

"They won't get far," Baca said. "I have their license numbers, and I'll call in a bulletin right now. If they're anywhere in California or Nevada, we'll have them by tonight."

The sheriff went back to Horton's body and began giving directions. One of the deputies pulled out a laptop computer and began taking notes, while another photographed the body before cutting it down. Gordon limped a few feet over to the creek and watched the water swirl gently through the meadow. Although it was not yet nine o'clock, it was already warm, and the day would probably be hot. An infrequens hatch was getting under way, the insects buzzing gently through the air, and he heard a splash to his left. He looked downstream and a few seconds later saw and heard a trout rise to an insect near the opposite bank. Ordinarily, the sight would have quickened his pulse, and sent him scurrying for his fly rod, but now he felt drained, empty and exhausted.

Then he had another thought, and his adrenaline kicked in. Gordon moved across the meadow as quickly as his bad ankle would let him, and found Baca jotting down some notes by his car.

"Something just came to me," Gordon said.

"Another hunch?"

"You could call it that. What if Radio and his men haven't left Summit County?"

"What do you mean?"

"The mine. If that's where they headed, we're in trouble. Once they get that stuff out of there, they'll have enough firepower to hold the whole county hostage."

Baca grabbed his car phone and began punching numbers.

• • •

Ten minutes after Baca's first phone call, Bill Boyd had two dozen agents from the Bureau of Alcohol, Tobacco and Firearms at Twin Creek Ranch. They found the vehicles from Radio's encampment on the perimeter road around the great meadow and cut the fuel lines to disable them. Joined by four Highway Patrol officers, they advanced on the mine, and arrived just as several men began to emerge from it, carrying boxes of munitions. A quick flurry of gunfire was exchanged, as Radio and his men retreated to the mine. Owing, perhaps, to nerves on both sides, no one was hit.

By the time Baca, his deputies, Gordon, and Sam arrived an hour later, a standoff was in effect. ATF agents covered the entrance to the mine from a clump of trees across the creek, 75 yards away. Two helicopters circled overhead, providing a steady drone of background noise. Several law-enforcement vehicles had been driven as close to the scene as possible without being put into the line of fire from the mouth of the mine, and Baca's county-issue Chevrolet Blazer joined them when he arrived. The SWAT team from Reno had been summoned in a mutual-aid call and was expected by one o'clock.

It turned out there had been another close call at the ranch that morning. Four men had burst into the main house, looking to take Ellen McHenry hostage, and had pistol-whipped a ranch foreman who was working in an office. Ellen, it turned out, had left moments earlier to visit Kitty in town, and had probably passed Radio's entourage on the highway, going the other direction. Baca reached her at Mom's Cafe on his car phone and confirmed that she was safe.

The sun was beating down relentlessly. It was already eighty degrees in the shade, and in the open, where Baca, Gordon and Sam were, the heat was perishing. A palpable tension settled over the waiting men, growing with each passing moment. Finally, Gordon approached Baca.

"What are you going to do?" he asked.

"Me? Not a damn thing, and I think Boyd feels the same. We can wait."

"You're just going to sit here until they come out?"

"Let me put it this way," Baca said. "We can send out to McDonald's for food. They can't. That's going to force their hand. And I'm willing to wait here until first snow if need be. Which reminds me. It's almost time for lunch, and since these men are likely to be here for a while, I need to feed them."

Fifteen minutes later, Ellen showed up, and Gordon hugged her. He told her the story of the morning, including the hanging of George Horton, how the men were cornered in the mine, and how they had broken into her house in an attempt to capture her. She shook her head.

"This is getting out of hand," she said.

At one o'clock, a white flag was poked outside the opening to the mine and waved around for a minute. A man emerged holding it and walked down to where the vehicles were parked. Gordon recognized him as Jason, the man with the knack for making a noose.

"I have a message for Sheriff Baca from Mr. Radio," he said. Baca stepped forward. "Mr. Radio would like the number of your car phone so he can talk to you and your word of honor as a gentleman that he won't be shot at if he steps out to call."

"He has my word," said Baca, taking a business card out of his shirt pocket and writing on it. "And here's the number. You can tell him I'm very anxious to have a word with him."

The messenger trudged back to the mine and disappeared inside it. A few moments later, Radio stepped out with a cellular phone in his hand and began punching numbers. The phone in Baca's car rang; it had a hands-free feature, and the sheriff pushed that button so that Gordon and the others clustered around the car could listen in on the conversation."

"This is Baca."

"Good afternoon, sheriff. Warm day, isn't it?"

"Get to the point, Radio."

"Do you have hands-free on your car phone? You don't seem to be holding anything." Baca was silent. "Only the best for your department, eh, sheriff? You're lucky to have such complacent taxpayers."

"You're wanted for questioning."

"Catch me if you can," Radio cackled. "Now why would that be?"

"You know good and well. I have a search warrant to look for a gun believed to be in your possession. And when you broke camp this morning, you left behind something I don't like to see. A dead body."

"If there'd been less of a hurry, we'd have cleaned up."

"Why did you do it, Radio?"

"There was no way around it, sheriff. George Horton killed one of the Brotherhood. By our code, he had to pay for it with his life."

"Did he admit to killing Dan McHenry?"

"Of course not. He denied it to the bitter end. But there was no getting around the facts. He had the gun; he had the opportunity; and he had the motive. Jealousy causes more murders than any other reason. Surely you know that. In your corrupt legal system, some pointy-headed lawyer could have stood the obvious on its head, but a people's posse can deal with the facts more directly."

"Where's that rifle?"

"In here with us. We felt we should be prepared to defend ourselves, and we turned out to be right. Those ATF people shot first and asked questions later."

"You're in a deep hole, Radio, in more ways than one. If I were you, I'd come out while there was still a chance of saving something from the situation."

Radio laughed. "I like your definition of chance."

Gordon slipped Baca a piece of paper. He looked at it and nodded.

"If you think that staying in there is going to protect anything, you're wrong. There were two people in that mine when George Horton and Hart Lee Bowen came in on Tuesday. We know you've found gold in there, and we know about the guns and explosives. We have a complete inventory on computer, and our list is probably better than yours."

Radio was silent for a moment. When he spoke again there was a hardness in his voice, and the mockery had gone out of it.

"I see," he said. "Well thank you, sheriff. Thank you for that information. It certainly gives us a little more to go on as we try to decide on our next move."

"Your next move should be to give up while there's still something an attorney can do for you. You may not like our legal system, but right now it's your best friend."

"We need some thinking time, sheriff. I'll get back to you if I have anything to say."

With that, Radio signed off, folded his phone, and ducked back into the mine.

• • •

Shortly before two o'clock, the first television crew and the Reno SWAT team arrived, in that order. Baca had left no one to guard the entrance to the ranch (a mistake he quickly rectified), and the television people — a camera man and a young reporter named Hunter George from one of the Reno stations — simply walked up to the sheriff's car and caught him unaware. Baca was not pleased.

"Get out of here," he growled.

"Wait a minute, sheriff, let's talk," said George. He was wearing a navy blazer with a pink striped shirt and a maroon patterned tie above blue jeans and running shoes. The viewing public never saw him below the waist, but from his belt up to his perfectly cut hair, he was turned out well.

"I'll talk, but not here," Baca said. "There are people up there with semiautomatic weapons. If you're anywhere around this area, you might end up in the line of fire. Go back to the entrance of the ranch, and I'll have someone come out and brief you on the hour."

"Is it true that Rex Radio is one of the men in the mine."

"Yes it is."

George whistled. "Then we're staying. You have the right to ask us to stay out of your way at a crime scene, but you can't just order us off the ranch."

Baca hesitated for a moment, weighing his desire to get rid of the reporters against the public relations implications of forcibly removing them. Ellen, who had been a few feet away during the discussion, came to his side.

"Excuse me, sheriff," she said, "but these people are trespassing on my property." She turned to the television men. "I'm going to ask you to leave. Since you're from Nevada, you may not understand California law, so let me explain it to you. If you trespass and are asked to leave by the property owner or an agent of the owner, you're subject to arrest." She smiled. "Sheriff Baca could probably spare a man for that, and you can't cover this story from jail."

George hadn't been expecting this. "All right," he said weakly.

"Look," said Baca, becoming conciliatory now that he had the upper hand, "I know you have your job to do, and I'm not trying to hold back information. I just don't want anybody to get hurt if I can help it. Wait at the entrance to the ranch, and I'll have somebody down there within an hour to brief you."

They went meekly, and Baca turned to Ellen. "Nice work," he said.

The SWAT team arrived moments later. Baca, Boyd, and the SWAT commander put their heads together and redeployed the men at their command. By carefully maneuvering their way into position, they were able to take cover in places that had them now surrounding the mine from every possible angle. There were about sixty officers and agents present by this time, and if Radio and his men had previously entertained any hope of making a break for freedom, that hope was now utterly dashed.

With the mine now covered and the helicopters still droning overhead, Baca went to the entrance of the ranch at three o'clock to face the news media. The original reporters had been joined by another TV crew from Reno, three from the Bay Area, two radio reporters, and a dozen print reporters and photographers. A standoff such as this would have been big news under any circumstances, but the involvement of Rex Radio made the story irresistible. By the time Baca went down for another briefing at five o'clock, there were nearly forty journalists waiting for him, with Associated Press and CNN now represented.

All afternoon, the heat never let up, and the angle of the sun was such that all those outside the mine spent several hours in its direct light. Gordon, Sam, and Ellen sat behind a patrol car, perspiration dripping down their faces and talking little.

"The sun should be behind the mountain in half an hour," Ellen said, when Baca left for the five o'clock news briefing.

"I could sure use a beer," Sam said.

"Same here," said Gordon. "What are we going to do, anyway? This could go on for days."

"Why don't we wait for sundown, then go back to the house if nothing's happened," Ellen said. "I can fix drinks and dinner."

"You're an angel," Sam said.

"We could take you out," Gordon offered.

She shook her head. "I'm not leaving the ranch until this is over."

"In one sense, though, it already is," Gordon said. "I mean, I'm not an attorney, but I can't see how Radio could possibly keep challenging the will. He has a charge of Murder One to contend with now. It looks as if the ranch will end up in the hands your father wanted it in."

"With a vein of gold thrown in to boot," Sam said.

"I'll believe that when I see it," Ellen said. "It sounds to me like wishful thinking on their part."

They were silent for a few moments, then she spoke again.

"Funny how much can happen in a week," she said to Gordon. "Just last Saturday my brother was alive and you, Kitty, the sheriff and I were having a barbecue with a hundred other happy people."

"It seems like forever," Gordon said.

"It's hard to make sense out of just what's happened in the last 24 hours," she said. "It may have been George Horton who pulled the trigger, but as far as I'm concerned, it's those men in the mine right now who killed my brother. They played on Dan's weakness and prejudice, and once he fell in with them, he was in real trouble. If it hadn't been for them, Dan and I could have worked something out about the ranch. I'm sure of that. But because they wanted it all, I had to fight."

"The fight's over at least," Gordon said.

"Once the sheriff gets hold of Dan's gun, that should settle the murder investigation," said Sam to Ellen. "That should be a load off your mind."

"The important thing from Ellen's perspective is that the missing gun was with them, not her." Gordon turned to her. "That's what was throwing suspicion toward you, and now you're off the hook."

She touched him on the knee. "You've done so much," she said.

"So have you."

By the time Baca returned from his news briefing, it was nearly six o'clock. The sun had gone behind the mountain enough to put the cars and trees on the east side of the creek in shade, while still illuminating the entrance to the mine.

"This could take a while," Baca said as he returned. I've sent a couple of men back to town for searchlights so we can light up the opening to the mine all night."

"Are you still going to wait it out?" Gordon asked.

"Do you have a better idea?"

"How long do you think it'll take?"

"It could be days, but I'm here for however long it takes. Whatever the cost in time and manpower, I won't feel we've succeeded until every last man in that mine comes out alive and is in the hands of the law."

"Do you think they'll give themselves up willingly?"

"I don't know," Baca said. "That's what I'm afraid of. They can't win if they try to fight it out, but they can make a hell of a mess and take some people with them. One thing, though, the longer they're in there, the better the odds they'll see where the percentages are."

"Look!" shouted Sam.

The sun had dropped lower, and the shadow of the mountain was now falling just below the entrance to the mine. A white flag had been pushed outside and was being waved around. After several seconds, it was withdrawn into the mine, and a moment later Radio stepped out. A cellular phone was in his right hand and what appeared to be a case of some sort was in the left.

He placed the latter on the ground and began calling. Baca moved to his car, drawing a crowd with him as the phone began to ring.

"Well, sheriff, you've got us," Radio said.

"I know that," Baca replied. "There are more than sixty armed men watching the opening to that mine. There's no way you can win a fight, Radio. Come out peacefully and let the attorneys take it from there."

"It's too bad, sheriff. If those men of yours had shown up just fifteen minutes later, we would have been combat-ready, and it would have been a different outcome. We've spent a lot of time practicing sniping from behind trees. Just like the original American patriots."

"And then what would you have done?"

"Let's just say we would have asserted ourselves. It was getting time to do that anyway, but circumstances pushed the schedule forward."

"Give up, Radio. You can't get out."

"We may not be able to get out, but you can't get in, and that's a consideration, too. We have some weapons that I'd hate to see fall into the wrong hands. And there's the gold in this mine. A rich vein of it. The society you represent, sheriff, is too corrupt to take possession of it.

Baca made no reply, but Gordon could see the anger in his eyes.

"No comment, sheriff? I don't blame you. What could you say? You stand for a society that has gotten away from what the founding fathers intended. You represent the fourteen-year-old girls who go out and have a second or third kid to bring in more welfare money. You represent the taxpayers who allow the government to take their hard-earned money and give it to people who don't work. You represent the decline and the decay of the American dream."

"And what, exactly, do you stand for, Radio? Besides hate and selfishness."

"You're wrong. I don't hate people as a rule; I'm just a realist. This country is being overrun by the nonproducers who are going to drive the real Americans into slavery if we don't stand up. Did you know, sheriff, that earlier this year there was a convention of gang members in Atlantic City? Six hundred leaders of youth gangs got together to plan something. The media didn't report it, of course, but it happened. I know. The Internet and the fax networks were full of reports about it. Where do you think the money for that convention came from? I'll tell you. It came from drug sales and welfare fraud, that's where."

"Did that really happen?" whispered Gordon.

Baca shrugged his shoulders while Radio went on with his monologue.

"And do you suppose for one minute, sheriff, that the outcome of that conference is going to be beneficial to you and me? You know the answer to that. If those people get together with a plan, there's going to be armed warfare in the streets of this country. Them against us. They have the weapons, and we have to match them, or we're doomed. The white people who made this country great are going to have to retreat to places like Summit County and make them fortresses against all the decay outside. We were going to be the first, but you stopped us. As far as I'm concerned, you're no better than they are."

"Thanks for the civics lesson," Baca said. "But you're in no position to move right now, let alone turn the tide of history. And there's a dead man at Sullivan Meadows you're going to have to answer for before your statue goes up in the civic plaza. You have no choice but to come out."

"Ah, but you're wrong, sheriff. You want us to surrender, and that'll never happen. We worked too hard to arm this people's militia, and we won't let our efforts fall into your hands. You see, there's another option besides surrender, and that's martyrdom. By making the ultimate sacrifice, we can call attention to our cause and inspire others to follow in our footsteps. We can do something glorious and noble and self-sacrificing that can change history. How many men ever get a chance to do that? We've been talking it over for several hours, and we agree on it to the last man. That's our decision."

"You're crazy," Baca said.

"And you're corrupt. See you in hell, brother."

The phone clicked off. Radio bent down to the box he'd carried out and touched it, then slipped, cat-like back into the mine shaft. The rapidly sinking sun had now left the entrance to it in shadow.

"Everybody on alert!" shouted Baca. "They may be pulling a Butch Cassidy. If they come out, anybody who shoots before they do is looking for a new job." He turned to Gordon and muttered, "Where are those damn spotlights? It's almost dark."

Then the music began, and Gordon realized that the object Radio had left by the entrance to the mine was a boom box. The tinny sound of The Star-Spangled Banner resounded through the dusk-infused air while everyone outside sat in tense anticipation, wondering that the fifteen people in the mine would do next. It was the same version Radio had played at camp the night before, and Gordon thought the song had never seemed so melancholy. He looked at the tensed figures around him, then back up to the entrance to the mine. As the music reached its crescendo, he softly sang to himself the final words, "O'er the land of the free and the home of the brave." For a full five seconds after the tape finished, the last bars of the music reverberated in the still mountain air.

Just as the last note faded out, there was a deafening explosion that sent an enormous cloud of dust and debris out the entrance of the mine. Rocks and pieces of wood flew through the air, landing in the grass and creek. Gordon was first startled, then stunned into insensibility. It took nearly a minute for him to realize all the implications of what had happened, and it took nearly that long for the echo from the explosion to go away. For another full minute, no one said a word, and many of the men looked on with eyes wide open and mouths agape. It was Baca who finally broke the silence.

"Jesus Christ," he said.

Interlude: Thursday September 30

(From today's edition of the Summit County Echo)

Last Friday, a week after the horrible tragedy that thrust Summit County into the national spotlight, Sheriff Mike Baca called off the search for fifteen men missing and presumed dead following an explosion in an abandoned mine located at the McHenry Ranch.

"We've been at it for a week and gotten nowhere," Baca said. "The walls of that mine are unstable as can be, and I'm not going to put the life and limb of my deputies at further risk trying to recover those bodies, or what's left of them."

The men were part of a paramilitary organization headed by Rex Radio, an ultraconservative former talk show host in San Francisco, whose program was ultimately removed from the air when he made remarks offensive from a racial and religious viewpoint. Radio's self-proclaimed "people's posse" had stockpiled an enormous cache of weapons and explosives in the mine, and according to Sheriff Baca, they were planning to remove and use the cache when confronted by law enforcement authorities late in the morning of Friday Sept. 17.

The result was a standoff with local officers and federal agents that lasted the remainder of the day. Shortly before sunset, Radio engaged law enforcement personnel in a rambling telephone conversation, at the close of which he said he and his men intended to be martyrs to their cause. The explosion occurred about five minutes after that conversation.

"We're going on the assumption that they detonated the explosives with suicidal intent," Baca said, "though it's possible they might have gone off by mistake. We know what was in there, and it wouldn't have taken much to set it off."

Interest in the shocking event was only heightened by the involvement of a personality of Radio's notoriety. Up until Tuesday of this week, representatives of the national news media have been in Summit County covering the story, and every motel in Harperville was filled to capacity each night.

In addition to capturing the national imagination, the standoff on the McHenry ranch brought about the conclusion of the investigation into the murder of Daniel McHenry, son of the late cattleman Frank McHenry. The younger McHenry had been shot to death while fishing on the family ranch Sunday Sept. 12.

Sheriff Baca said in a news conference this week that a rifle missing from the McHenry family home, and now believed to be the murder weapon, had been positively identified as being at the encampment maintained by Radio and his followers at Sullivan Meadows on the West Fork of the Buchanan River.

In serving a search warrant at that location Friday Sept. 17, Baca discovered that the group had pulled up camp and left behind the body of one of their members, George Horton, 32, a close friend of the late Daniel McHenry. Horton was found hanging lifelessly from a tree, a rope around his neck.

During the standoff later that day, Radio blamed Horton, who had possession of the weapon in question, for the killing of young McHenry and said that Horton had been "executed" for his alleged role in that death.

"We're operating on the premise that George Horton or someone else in the Rex Radio encampment committed the crime," Baca said at his Tuesday news conference. "There is no evidence whatsoever linking anyone else to it, and we have therefore closed the books on our investigation."

The gun in question was with Radio and his followers when the explosion occurred, and, like them, has been permanently entombed.

"The morning after the murder of Dan McHenry, we asked for permission to search their camp, and it was denied," Baca said. "We had no cause to ask for a warrant until Friday of that week. If we had been able to locate that rifle the day after the shooting, there are 16 men who would be alive today, and a great many innocent people would have been spared a lot of pain."

Finally, the events of Sept. 17 have had one more effect. On Monday of this week, the trial over the McHenry will came to court after two continuances. Manfred Bosso, San Francisco attorney representing Daniel McHenry, moved to dismiss his challenge to the will, and Judge Hawkins accepted the motion.

Bosso explained in court that Daniel McHenry had drawn up a will leaving his estate to Rex Radio, who had planned to continue the challenge. With Radio's presumed death in the mine explosion, any right to continue the challenge fell to his designated beneficiary, the American Militia Foundation.

The Foundation notified Bosso that it would not pursue the challenge to the will, but would be content to accept Daniel McHenry's annual share of income from the ranch, as provided in the will that was being challenged. With Frank McHenry's last will now uncontested, the ranch, its stock, and its improvements, which constitute the bulk of the estate, will go to his daughter, Ellen, thus making good his dying wish.

Probate is expected to take several months. Miss McHenry, who has been sorely tried by the death of two family members this year, not to mention the legal struggle over her father's will, has temporarily taken leave of Summit County. She is reportedly staying with a friend in San Francisco and could not be reached for comment.

Epilogue: Monday July 18, 1994

The clock outside the First National Bank of Summit County read 2:28 as Gordon drove by, and the temperature was a cool 72 degrees, owing to the thunderstorm that was rapidly bearing down on Harperville. Rumblings could be heard in the distance, but it had not yet begun to rain. When he pulled up in front of Mom's Cafe, it was 2:30, closing time. As he got out of the Cherokee, he couldn't help remembering that it was almost ten months to the day since the cataclysmic standoff at the McHenry ranch.

He walked through the door and was relieved to see that the last customer of the day was paying his check. Kitty's eyes lit up as she saw Gordon, and she ran over and hugged him as the customer walked out the door.

"Gordon! What a surprise," she said. "It's good to see you."

"Same here." He looked around. On the face of it, the cafe appeared to be the same as the last time he visited, but something was different, and he couldn't put his finger on it.

"I'm officially closed, but for you I can whip up some lunch."

"Please don't bother. I'm fine. If you have any coffee, though, I wouldn't mind a cup."

"You bet. The last pot's still pretty fresh. Sit down and I'll be right back."

She went behind the counter, detouring along the way to turn over the sign by the front door so that the "Closed" side was facing outward. She returned with two cups of coffee, and put cream into hers. Gordon drank his black.

"So what have you been up to?" she asked.

"Taking it easy," he said. "Smelling the flowers."

"Lucky you. But what does taking it easy mean?"

"I stay on top of my investments. That takes an hour or two a day. I do more traveling and fishing. And lately

I've been working as a consultant to nonprofit organizations in the Bay area."

"How interesting!"

"It is. There are a lot of people out there dedicating themselves to good work, and I really respect them. But too often they don't know how to run the details of their organization. So I show them how to set up their books and track their money and use their computers to the best advantage."

"Do you get paid for that?"

Gordon smiled. "I work for a flat fee of ten dollars, which is enough money for a beer and a tip at the best watering holes in San Francisco. I charge that just to remind them that they're getting something of value, but in essence, I'm donating my time."

He sipped his coffee, swallowed, and took a deep breath.

"So how's Ellen?"

"She's fine," said Kitty. "She's been working really hard on the ranch, and after all the excitement last year, things are starting to get back to normal."

"She had enough excitement last year to last a lifetime."

"I don't think even you know what she went through."

"Obviously not. I suppose you're wondering what happened with us?"

"I've heard her story."

"That's probably pretty accurate."

"I don't know. She was upset and confused about it herself. Are you going to see her, now that you're here again?"

"I don't think so."

"You should give it a second chance. She'd be glad to see you."

"I'd love to see her, too, but it may not be a good idea." He got up and walked to the window while he collected his thoughts. "We had two wonderful months in San Francisco. I can always remember that. She enjoyed the city life much more than I thought she would. She got along with my friends, of course, and they all loved her. In fact, I'm avoiding Sam right now because whenever we get together, I have to spend half the time listening to him tell me what a mistake I made.

"But all that time there was a tension running beneath the surface. You know, in the movies, they always have two people falling in love during some incredible adventure, and that's what happened to us. But I think in real life, that sort of abnormal situation distorts the relationship."

Outside the rain had begun falling. As is often the case in the mountains, it came down in sheets immediately, with no preliminaries.

"She really appreciates what you did," Kitty said. "You risked your life for her."

Gordon took his coffee cup behind the counter and refilled it.

"I'm sure she appreciates it, but you know something, Kitty? I think at some level she resents it, too. Ellen's a wonderful woman, but she's too proud to feel she owes a man something — even though Sam and I owe our lives to her shooting ability."

"She said you were withdrawn, like you were holding in some demon you couldn't bear to let loose."

Gordon sat at the table again. "She's very perceptive. I couldn't tell her, but I have to tell you." He looked Kitty in the eyes. "You see, I know who killed Dan McHenry."

Kitty said nothing for a few seconds, and when she spoke it was in a flat voice. "I thought that was settled," she said.

"In a sense it is. But I have to tell somebody, and you're the only one I can."

"Go on."

"You gave yourself away the day afterward," Gordon said. "When Sam and I were having lunch here and talking about the murder, you said, 'A thirty-ought six could make a real mess out of a man.' I didn't notice it at the time, but a few days later when I was reading the newspaper story and came to the part where Baca wasn't saying what kind of gun was used, I remembered. Aside from the sheriff, Ellen McHenry and myself, only one other person could have known then what caliber rifle was used to shoot Dan McHenry. The person who killed him."

The rain was coming down even more furiously now, and they listened to it for a full minute before Kitty spoke.

"That's hardly proof, you know. As close as I was to the family, I could have known what caliber Dan's gun was."

"Maybe, but once I realized that, everything else fell into place. Dan McHenry's killer had to know he'd be fishing on the ranch. You were there the night before when Ellen announced it, and you were really upset. You were close to a surrogate mother for her, and you resented the fact that Dan was trying to undo Frank McHenry's will, at Ellen's expense. You knew losing the ranch would devastate Ellen. A lot of crimes have been committed with less motive than that.

"You also knew the ranch well enough to duck down that road and get in position. You don't have an alibi for that morning. You weren't at the cafe when we were there for breakfast, and you weren't home when Ellen called on you at the time of the shooting. What's more, you're a deer hunter who knows how to use a rifle. Everyone says you're a crack shot. You had what Baca says he always looks for — motive, means and opportunity. It all fits."

Kitty was looking vacantly past Gordon, her face pale. When she spoke, it was in a barely audible croak.

"I wondered for days afterward if you picked up on that and might try to make something out of it." She paused and stared into her coffee cup. "You know, last year was the first time in thirty years I didn't go deer hunting. Funny, all of a sudden, I just couldn't bring myself to do it."

Then Gordon realized what was different in the cafe. The deer head that had hung on the wall by the front door was no longer there.

"Too bad we'll never know what would have happened if Dan McHenry lived," he said.

"Don't be a sentimental jackass. He'd have won the lawsuit, and he and Radio and that gang would be playing soldier on the McHenry ranch right now while Ellen was scraping by and trying to pay her legal bills. It's too bad it happened the way it did, but with the people he was involved with, he wasn't going to live to a ripe old age, anyway. Not with Rex Radio as the beneficiary of his will."

"You may be right, but still ..."

"You realize, don't you, that if your theory is right, you risked your life for nothing when you went out looking for Dan's gun. And you realize that you're accusing me of putting Ellen in danger of being arrested for murder. Do you really think I would do that?"

"No," said Gordon, "I think if it had come to that, you would have done something. It's funny — although no one was laughing at the time — how a whole set of random circumstances conspired to make Ellen look guilty. You gave her time to get to town so she'd have an alibi, but she went to your place, so she didn't have one. If Dan had told Ellen he was taking his gun, or if she had noticed it earlier instead of having Baca find a gap in the gun rack, she wouldn't have been flustered and confused and drawn suspicion on herself. And what were the odds that rifle would be the same caliber as yours?"

"So what are you going to do now?"

Gordon took a sip of coffee and tried to frame his words carefully.

"Let me put it this way. You're not the only one in this affair who's carrying a load of guilt. I still wake up in the middle of the night, thinking about George Horton dangling from that tree. He wouldn't have ended up there if I hadn't pointed Radio toward that rifle and as much as said George was the killer. You killed a man directly, but I caused one to be killed."

"But he would have died in the mine, anyway."

"They wouldn't have been in the mine that day if they hadn't hanged him. Besides, I think he was getting ready to walk out on that bunch, and if things hadn't come to a head so fast, he might have done it. Then there's the other situation. It wasn't more than ten seconds after that explosion that I realized the position I was in. Only I knew about what you'd said. If Baca had recovered Dan McHenry's gun, I could have let him figure things out for himself. But with the evidence buried for all eternity, it was up to me to come forward. Against all teaching and inclination, I didn't."

"Why?"

"Because it would have devastated Ellen and made a bad situation worse. If I told Baca what I knew, he would have acted on it, and there would have been no end to the nightmare for Ellen. I hope I did the right thing by leaving well enough alone, but right or not, that was my decision, and I'm not about to change it now. But I had to let you know, which is why I came by today."

"Are you going to be around for a while?"

Gordon shook his head. "I'd better not. I was deeply in love with Ellen, but that's over now. What I know would come between us, as sure as can be. And what I know will make Summit County an uncomfortable place to be for a long time to come. I have a week off, and I'm going to spend it north of here." Gordon rose. "Tell her I was by and asked about her, OK?"

Kitty nodded. "Thanks for sharing your interesting theory with me," she said, "and thanks for not sharing it with anyone else."

"Remember why," he said.

Kitty stood up, took Gordon's right hand between hers and gave it a solid squeeze. Without another word, he walked out the door. As he left Harperville, he thought that Kitty was probably on the phone now, and he wondered what she was telling Ellen.

He drove north out of town, past the Stage Stop Restaurant, and up the winding road to the top of the pass. The thunderstorm had been of short duration, and when he reached the summit, the rain had stopped entirely, though the dark clouds could be seen moving east. Pulling into a turnout he got out, and gazed down on the valley and the town far below. He made it a long look, because he knew it would be the last one for some time to come. As the events of last September flashed through his mind, a powerful feeling of loss began to grip his body, freezing him where he stood. It took all his will power to shake it off, walk back to the car and start the engine. As he drove down the other side of the pass, with Haperville now out of sight, he could feel the tension draining from his body. He was headed north, to places he'd never been before, and there was, after all, a week of fishing ahead.

Photo by gregpio.com

MICHAEL WALLACE has been reading mysteries since he got hooked on Agatha Christie's *Murder in Mesopotamia* at the age of 12. He has been fly fishing, with varying degrees of success, for 30 years. The two interests have converged in his first novel, *The McHenry Inheritance.*

When not reading mysteries or fishing, he was a reporter and editor for a daily newspaper for 19 years and now has a public relations/publication consulting business. He lives in Santa Cruz County, CA.

Contact Michael Wallace through his website, quillgordonmystery.com